Indian Summer

Short Fiction

Kristina Baer

ISBN – 978-1-953120-86-1

Distributed by Ingram Books

Contents

Indian Summer

Alice

Kneeling beside the bed of hostas, she clips leaves and stems laid waste by slugs. Over the years, she had tried every antidote known to chemists and old wives to halt their annual onslaught. To no avail. Now, at the first sign of Indian summer, she devotes time every morning to this task, doubling the size of her compost pile by summer's end. Next spring, as she does every year, she'll dig the mixture into the border to nourish next year's plants. ("And slugs," Ted teased.)

The noon siren blares from the fire station a mile away. Sitting back on her heels, Alice wipes her face with a shirttail. Behind her, the garden gate slams shut. Lying nearby, Sheba woofs softly.

She stands to greet Steve Carlson, her realtor and Ted's tennis partner, who hugs her and bends over to kiss her cheek. "Great day to show the place, no?" At ease with himself and the world, Steve is comfortable with his height and his girth. Usually fastidious about his appearance, today his shirt is rumpled, the armpits soaked. He pulls at his collar. Alice smiles, hoping to reassure him. "Fran cleaned yesterday. She even put out some sunflowers." *I hope they like sunflowers.*

Steve smiles. He had promised her a quick sale. Then, when the market turned two months ago, he reassured her. "It's a special house, Alice. Someone looking for an authentic, unspoiled historic home will show up." He nodded at the dogwoods at the upper end of the lawn. "Just in time!"

Alice and Ted had planted the trees thirty years ago, the first spring after they bought the house. Now, nearly mature, their foliage begins to turn at the onset of cooler weather, usually at the first frost announcing Indian Summer. They keep their deep-red leaves well into winter. Steve had joked that she must have some Pequot blood. "Or possibly some Narragansett?" she joked back. The nurseryman had told her that this variety of dogwood had been cultivated by regional Indians. Which tribe was responsible was the mystery. Alice had decided to credit the Narragansetts, one of the oldest tribes in North America, who had occupied most of what is now Rhode Island.

At first, she and Steve had dissected every showing. No longer. Alice had realized that most of the people who came to see the house were looking for a carefree second home in Newport, not a quirky antique. He has told her that the people coming today know a lot about 18th-century houses and are "serious buyers." By now she knows better than to get her hopes up.

Steve always stops by to check in before he shows the house. Like a good stage manager, he knows this attention eventually will reap a payoff. Alice has heard the story about the broken pipe he discovered several hours before showing a house to a demanding client. Pipe repaired, the plumber was long gone when Steve arrived with the buyer—who offered "full asking." He knows each of his properties well, knows how to judge a buyer's interests and when—and how—to reveal critical information. He is also practiced at reading "buy signals." In the case of Alice's house, there haven't been many of those.

"I'll meet them at the office," he says now. "Should be back soon."

Had he told her their name? If so, she has forgotten it. For now, until—if—they make an offer, she doesn't need it. "One o'clock?"

"Yeah. At least I think so. They were supposed to confirm, but I haven't heard back yet."

"OK, then. I'll go in soon. We'll be... I'll be ready, don't worry."

"Alice, I know... I mean, this isn't..."

"Go meet your clients, Steve. I'm OK." He pats her shoulder and leaves.

There would be open houses in the neighborhood today. Alice knows which properties are competing with hers. She knows their shortcomings. Sometimes, lying awake at night, she lists the pluses and minuses, "us" versus "them." This is pointless, she realizes. To her, this house is so much more than a house, its "whole" so much greater than a sum of its parts.

When she decided to sell, she hadn't considered talking to other realtors. Ted and Steve had been friends for 40 years, longer than she and Ted had been married, and that was reason enough to hire him. Now, Alice realizes, working with Steve has become a way to keep Ted present in her decision. Even now, two years after Ted's death, Steve finds ways to mention him in their conversations, as if Ted were only away for a day or two, as if her decisions mattered to him still. Also, Steve understands the house and appreciates the garden. With Steve in charge, the formalities are merely items on a checklist, to be gone through one by one. This frame of mind helps her not to care so much when she observes the slight disarrangement of furniture or objects caused by strangers passing through, or the lingering smell of an unfamiliar perfume. Or when Steve reports to her a negative comment, "the ceiling is too low" or "the floorboards are crooked."

Just before he died, she and Ted had talked for the last time about selling the house. "Don't think about it as a deal," he told her.

"I don't want to think about it at all."

"I know, sweetheart, but you need to decide if you want to stay or go."

"I can't." Then, "You're the one who's going." She hugged him. "Sorry, sorry...so sorry..." Stretched out beside him in bed, she moved closer, feeling his breath against her hair, thinking, *How much longer?*

"You could go up to Vermont, find something near Annie..." he pushed away, tilting his head to look into her eyes. She sat up, leaving his unspoken question unanswered, knowing he wouldn't have suggested this before.

They had talked occasionally about what each would do if the other died first. Talking about dying was just another opportunity to do what they did best—discuss options, figure out a plan, and move on. But when Ted's prognosis became clear, she felt paralyzed. Ted's suggestion that she move to Vermont was his way of telling her he had admitted to himself—and accepted—the finality of this separation. Then, she would not accept it, steeling herself intellectually and emotionally against it. Now, she believes that if she takes Ted's suggestion to move to Vermont, near Annie, fulfilling his dream for them, it will help keep her memories alive. Her relationship with Annie would take its own course, carried along in the current of their shared memories of Ted.

Throughout his life, Ted's generosity had been the hallmark of everything he did. A talented inventor, he filled notebooks with ideas, observations, and sketches of anything that caught his eye. Early in their marriage, as their house filled with books, odds and ends, collections, and projects in progress—objects in bottles, scrapbooks of clippings and photographs—Alice had put on mental blinders. The alternative—building a workshop for Ted on their narrow lot—would have meant giving up her garden. Besides, she loved his amplitude, and found refuge in it. So, she learned to work around his passions. Once infused with wonder and joy, after he died these vestiges of Ted's energy and talent lay inert, gathering dust, until at last Alice dismantled and sorted them, piece by piece, saving what she could salvage, disposing of the rest.

The garden testifies to her management of constraints, of working with them and making them work for her. Her hosta collection is one of the largest in the area. Her peonies win awards every year. Although she hasn't put it on the summer tour for years, people who have visited her garden in the past always stop by to see how it has developed since their last tour. Some have become close friends. As much as she had loved Ted and the house, it is the garden that completes her, the garden that anchors and sustains her in the world. It will survive her departure, she knows.

The condo she had found in Manchester, Vermont, has a small patio, with room for a reasonable selection of potted plants. Annie now lives in Bennington, far enough away to make drop-in visits unlikely. Now fifty-nine, Alice anticipates running her life according to her own whims, free to do what she wants, when she wants. So far, Annie has gone along with her plans. Alice recognizes this situation likely will change once she is established in her new place.

Like her father, Annie is large-boned and generous, her energy and enthusiasms all-encompassing. Unlike her father, she doesn't understand Alice, believing that she'll eventually come around, like a willful child who refuses to do something until she realizes it is fun. Alice suspects that Annie, who has friends in Manchester, already has a list of people to introduce her to, maybe even a few eligible men.

Gathering up her gardening tools, Alice hears the gate slam, then voices.

Jack

"Should I take the next right? America's Cup?" Liz is driving. I'm reading the directions. She usually drives when the route is unfamiliar. Reading anything in the car makes her carsick.

"Yeah. That's good. You want to stay on America's Cup until we get to Memorial."

She glances at me. "Memorial? Isn't that a few lights down?"

"I see you've memorized the map..."

She laughs. "I remember that much from our trip here for Allen's funeral. Remember? We were late and ended up with a parking ticket." Stopped at the light, she looks at me. "I love this house, Jack. It's a lot like Mom's. You'll see." When I start to point out that this house resembles that one in age only, she adds, "We're just looking, sweetie. Don't panic."

I enjoy house-hunting. It makes a nice outing for us in the spring or early fall. Also, frankly, it satisfies the voyeur in me. I like to imagine the lives of the people who live in the houses we visit. But my interest usually stops there. I'm not eager to move again. Our five cross-country moves in thirty years have drained me of the enthusiasm I used to feel for beginning a new life in a new place. Liz is aware of this. But I know that if she finds a house she really likes, she will campaign against my resistance or wait me out. She feels me looking at her. We both smile.

"I know. There's no harm in looking," I say. This is usually her line. "But there is something called love at first sight." This reminder of how we found our present home provokes her.

"Jack…"

"Just joking. Really. I want to see this house, too. Who knows? Maybe Washington slept there." Her shoulders relax. Together, we glide back on track.

Once we reach the intersection of Memorial and Spring Street, I play my mental slide show of the house. Built in 1719, it's a story-and-a-half gambrel, about 1,800 square feet, on a 5,000 square-foot lot half a block from Newport Harbor. It has been restored, which means the original structure and floor plan are intact. Central chimney, original keeping room, and wide-board floors—it's nice enough. The thing is, you must love the idea of a house like this and live in it on its terms. It owns you. You become a curator or a conservator, committed to preservation in lieu of improvements. Liz loves this aspect. I do not. So, I am framing my questions about the house to get straight answers from the realtor and a home inspector.

At breakfast, Liz and I talked about what to ask the realtor. "It's fine to ask questions, Jack, but could you please try not to sound like the Grand Inquisitor?"

"You know how realtors are. The spec sheet isn't the whole story. If we're going to get into this, I want more."

"Well, of course. But let's at least take a good look before we start hammering the poor guy, OK?"

For Liz's sake, I'll give him a chance. But realtors—and home inspectors, for that matter—can be masters of equivocation and overstatement: Five more years on that cedar-shingle roof? Maybe, provided the New England fall is atypical and sparing of nor'easters. The cellar is "a little damp" after several days of rain? Check the water stains. And then there are the "charming quirks" that may or may not betray structural defects—the cracked floorboards, the fireplace that smokes when the wind blows from the west. You get the picture. Sellers are required to disclose certain conditions. For a three-hundred-year-old house like this one, this is almost always an exercise in futility.

Beyond the items on the spec sheet, this house has some problems, not all of which have to do with its age. For instance, it's in the coastal flood plain. Sure, being half a block from Newport Harbor is appealing. Still, I believe what I read about climate change and its potential effect on hurricane strength, so buying a house in a vulnerable location doesn't make a whole lot of sense to me. Insurance is available, but what sensible person buys a home that stands a reasonable chance of being inundated?

I've kept my counsel. I know that if I mention these objections to Liz, I'll be opening the conversation to a knock-down drag-out discussion of my "propensity to look for trouble."

I indicate to Liz the realtor's sign ahead on the left. In front of us, a car pulls into the parking lot. We pull in next to it. As I get out, I hear Liz greet the driver. It's Steve Carlson, the broker Liz has talked to. "...about one o'clock," he's saying. I look at my watch: It's 12:45.

"We can go over there now, if you like," Steve tells us. "Let me pick up the brochure and specs for you." Liz gathers her bag and camera from our car.

On our way, Liz sits in the front seat of Steve's car. He does the talking, explaining about the house and the circumstances of the sale—the husband's death, the wife's decision to move to Vermont. When we pull up across from the house, I see that it sits perpendicular to the street on the sidewalk, its front entrance hidden behind a six-foot fence. This is unusual and surprising: In the 18th century, given contemporary street conditions, you would not have wanted to walk around the house from the street to its front door. From the street, the house looks much smaller than the specs indicate. With no shutters or window boxes to clutter its simple lines, it reflects the modesty and sobriety of the ship's carpenter who built it. The roof's cedar shingles are weathered, but intact. Liz catches my eye.

There is no driveway, so we park on the street and enter through the front gate. The six-foot cedar fence that encloses the lot is a violation of city ordinances, I'm sure. But it doesn't feel like a spite fence.

An irregular fieldstone path runs the length of the lot. Borders of perennials in bloom and a variety of trees, including dogwoods and maples, accentuate its depth and breadth. It is an exquisite private park. Thanks to the broad canopies of several large maples, it is much cooler here. A light breeze ruffles the leaves, already bearing the golds and reds of early Indian Summer. At the far end of the lawn, the largest maple—thirty or forty feet tall? — lifts its mammoth limbs to the sky, casting shadows both mysterious and reposeful over the border gardens and lawn.

A woman kneels in the shade, her head turned toward us, one hand resting on the shoulder of a dog lying beside her in the grass. Liz and I wait by the front steps, watching Carlson as he speaks to her.

Alice

When the front door closes behind Steve and his clients, she relaxes. Finished or not, she has had enough for today. Sipping water from her thermos, she ignores her hunger pangs and stretches out. Gradually, the tension between her shoulders eases. For as long as she can remember, she has loved to lie in the grass, looking up into and through the branches and leaves, which seem pinned to the sky, holding it in place. It reminds her of the tulip trees in Princeton's Marquand Park, whose height and proportions captivated her the summer she spent working on her dissertation.

That had been a foul, humid summer. She had spent most days in the air-conditioned library, studying for her second field exam, while Jack did research for his dissertation and prepared his course for fall semester. Sundays were reserved for early lovemaking, a late breakfast, an afternoon movie.

Weekdays, walking up Witherspoon Street to get to the campus by 8:00 had been like swimming in brackish water. The shade cast by the trees along the street offered no relief. The cloying fragrance of blooming privet mingled thickly with the scorched smell of pavement and car exhaust.

When she had finished her first year of graduate work, her parents had urged her to live at home. With barely enough in her teaching stipend to buy groceries, let alone pay rent, she had considered their offer, then declined, because she and Jack had decided to live together. She hadn't told her parents.

They were about to give up when they found an apartment on Witherspoon Street, a house-sitting arrangement. The couple who lived in the apartment needed a cat-sitter while they travelled in Europe. Rent-free, it would tide them over until they could move back into graduate housing in September.

Mornings, they walked to the campus together. They met at the end of the day, at home, where she usually prepared dinner. Since most of their friends were away, they were apart only when they were studying. At first, Alice welcomed the intimacy, their calm domesticity a striking contrast to the turbulence she had known growing up. But that summer, she could feel how deeply Jack needed her to be who he wanted her to be. The more she understood this, the more she disengaged from him.

When her emotions threatened to override her self-control, she gathered them up, smoothed them down, evened them out, to make herself the person he thought he loved. In time, she understood how frightened she had been of commitment, especially in a relationship defined by someone else's needs. And Jack needed her, leaned on her, depended on her.

One evening they argued. She can still hear the screen door, the double thud it made as he left the house. They had been talking about his research. He was describing a new article he had read, one that gave him a good way to frame his discussion of the text he was writing about. Like her, he was a medievalist. Unlike her, he had a head for dry, punctilious scholarship and enjoyed the traditional (to her, stultifying) forms of scholarly debate. He was about to drive his point home when she giggled. He flushed and stood up, knocking over his full wine glass.

"What? What's so funny?" They had rarely disagreed, let alone argued; their relationship was that new.

"You know..." she began.

"What?" he demanded.

"Why are you so set on beating up this guy, the one who wrote the article? Why is that so important to you? What are your ideas, anyway? It seems like this is more about ego bashing. The guy is dead, Jack."

"That's enough, Alice."

"I'm not finished."

"I am." The back door slammed behind him.

Later, she found him in Marquand Park, lying in the grass. The new moon dangled in the branches of a nearby tulip tree.

Lying beside him, she whispered, "I'm sorry." They had made love, there in the grass.

She had dropped out at the end of fall term.

Jack

In the entry, Jack waits for his eyes to adjust to the dimness. Alert, anticipating, he inhales the fragrance, a mixture of lavender, wood smoke, dust, damp stone, and furniture wax. Just ahead of him, opposite the front door, three uneven risers begin the spiral stairs from the entry to the second floor. To his right is the keeping room, now the dining room. The living room is to his left. Steve Carlson is talking about the central chimney, whose four fireplaces—two in the upstairs bedrooms, and the two down in the keeping room and the living room—once provided heat for the whole house. "As you might imagine, in cold weather they kept the fires burning day and night."

Liz asks a question. Jack steps into the keeping room toward the kitchen, a recent addition, where a walk-in fireplace occupies most of one wall. Sunlight pours into the room from a skylight. The wide-pine floor glows. Framed and hanging over the mantlepiece are several hand-colored lithographs. Each shows a French scene, identified by place name. Judging from their size, these are illustrations from a travel guide, probably one from the nineteenth century. He takes a closer look at the river scene labeled Chalôns-sur-Saône, which shows cargo-laden, flat-bottom boats, propelled by oarsmen, reflected in the calm, transparent blue water. On the quay, a couple—he in a top hat and dark red formal coat, she in a blue gown, hair upswept—stands looking out at the scene. A small dog prances on its hind legs in front of them.

"Doesn't it look like a Sunday afternoon, like they're taking a stroll after lunch?" Alice leaned against him. Because the print was small, no more than 5" x 7", the heads of the figures in the print were almost touching.

"More likely late afternoon, I think. Look how long their shadows are." It sometimes irritated her that he paid attention to details like this. But she was looking intently at the figures themselves.

"I love that he's touching her arm," she had said.

"He's probably courting her, showing her his ship has come in—it really looks like he's gesturing toward that barge, the one with the cargo heaped on it, doesn't it?"

"Yeah, but check out the sky. Could be some weather on the way!" She said this in a light imitation of her father, a sailor. They spent a few more minutes looking at other illustrations, then went to a nearby café for a drink. Alone, he later returned to the shop and bought the print, which he gave to her for her birthday.

All these years later, he recognizes the print's obvious symbolism. How else to view the couple beneath the gathering storm clouds, except through the lens of his disastrous relationship with Alice? He is drawn back to the past, back to the enigmatic woman he had loved and lost.

They had met on the bus to New York when she sat next to him in the last available seat. After exchanging pleasantries, they had fallen easily into conversation as they idled in the late afternoon traffic on the New Jersey Turnpike. She had just applied to Princeton, to do graduate work in French. He was in his first year there—in French. She had a beautiful voice. Glancing at her profile, he had been bewitched by the arch of her eyebrow, the swell of her lower lip. Was she pretty? He closes his eyes, sees her again as she was then.

She was beautiful.

A month later, signing the purchase and sale papers, Alice is certain Steve is unaware that she knew Jack—that she had known Jack. Had Jack revealed he had known her? Surely Steve would have mentioned it.

"Are you OK?" Steve asked. "Is it too warm in here?"

She put the paper she had just signed on top of the pile and sat back. "Could I have some water?"

"Of course." Steve left the room and returned with a bottle of water and a glass.

Alice smiled and sighed. "So much paperwork for one little house."

Steve handed her the last batch of forms.

Driving north that afternoon, Alice called and told Annie everything.

Annie

From the porch window, she watches the car turn into the driveway. "She's here now." Annie steps back into the kitchen, toward the phone.

"So that's all you know about this guy? That she knew him in graduate school? I bet they were lovers."

"Josie!"

"Well, it's plausible, isn't it?" Josie laughs.

"Gotta go. She's getting out of the car."

The trunk gapes open. Like the Volvo's backseat, it is crammed with odds and ends. Alice has already removed and stacked several bags and beach towels on the lawn.

"Let me help, Mom."

Alice gestures at the piles. "Can you believe all this stuff?" She rummages in the trunk and pulls out a Teddy bear and a child's blanket, its edges bound in blue. She holds both out to Annie. "He was wrapped up in it at the bottom of the blanket chest."

"You gave him to me for my fifth birthday."

"And you insisted on calling him 'Teddy'." Alice smiles. "Your Dad even invented a special voice for him."

Annie hugs the bear. "This is it, Teddy. You're home at last."

Later, over dinner, Alice tells Annie about Jack, about being a year behind him in graduate school, about leaving Princeton after her first year. "I loved French, loved teaching. But I wasn't cut out to be a scholar." She laughs. "I needed air."

"What are your plans now?"

Alice shrugs. "I'm going to give myself a year or so to figure that out." She pauses.

"What?"

"Remember the woman I told you about? The woman who lives in the same neighborhood in Manchester?"

"The gardener?"

Alice nods. "I'm thinking about working with her on some of her projects, at least helping out with maintenance." She doesn't have to tell Annie how much she will miss her Newport garden.

The next morning, as they're finishing breakfast, a truck pulls up and brakes in front of the house. "I'll go see who that is," Annie says. Alice begins to clear the table.

"Mom?"

Alice dries her hands and heads outside, where Annie stands in the driveway. She gestures at the truck, its loading ramp now positioned on the sidewalk. "It's a delivery for you from the local nursery."

"Right on time." Alice smiles. She signs the delivery papers, and hands the envelope to the driver, who wheels a dolly loaded with two pots off the truck, and heads up the driveway toward the back of the house. "Just a minute, please?" Alice interjects. "Could you put that pot here on the sidewalk beside the Volvo?" She gestures at the smaller of the two pots. "The other one goes in the back of the house."

"Mom?" Annie leans over the plant on the sidewalk, checking the tag. "Cornus Racimosa? I don't recognize it."

"It's a gift from your Dad. And from the Newport house," Alice tells her. "Let's put it in back. I'll tell you all about it."

At the kitchen table, with a fresh cup of coffee, Alice smooths open the information brochure attached to Annie's plant. "Cornus racimosa," she reads. "A variety of dogwood. Grows to 10 feet. White flowers. Birds love its white berries. Red leaves in the fall." She looks at Annie.

"What?"

"I remember the day our two dogwoods arrived in Newport. That was thirty years ago." Alice smiles. "They were Dad's gift to the garden. He planted them where they'd have space to grow and plenty of light. Three-feet tall then. Now they've topped seven." Her voice caught.

"Do you remember the year the cardinals nested in the one by the house?"

"You were in fourth grade. You wanted so much to take the nest and the birds to school, for show and tell. How could I forget?" Alice laughs.

"I still have the slide show Dad made for me to take to school to show the class."

"I know I'll have to learn how to prune this plant. Otherwise, it will take over the patio." She shrugged. "Not sure if I'll have cardinals in Manchester. It's a different place, a different time."

"And a different plant," Annie said.

Keeping Secrets

Cirrus clouds feather the dark blue August sky; a stiff breeze raises whitecaps. The lone sailboat skims the lake, heeled over hard, its skipper almost invisible against the bright water. To the west, mountains climb steeply from the shore. To the north, a mass of cumulus clouds rises, their peaks challenging the mountains'. Running before the wind now, the sailboat is as insubstantial as milkweed silk.

Liz, Ellen, and Alice have known each other since college, where they met as freshmen. By affinity as much as by chance, they became friends and roommates. Through marriage, divorce, remarriage, financial and health worries, and the death of Liz's husband, Scott, four months ago, friendship has been their anchor to windward.

Liz still listens for Scott's footsteps, sets mail aside for him, and when she shops, buys foods that he liked, even anchovies, which she will never eat. The other day, a Carolina Wren perched in the dogwood outside the kitchen. "Scott, come quick!" Lying in a patch of sunlit floor, the dog raised her head and looked at Liz, then looked toward the door. When Scott didn't appear, she sighed and went back to sleep.

This June Thursday, they are on their way to spend a long weekend in Newport, a trip organized by Ellen and Alice to distract Liz. Reflecting now on what lies ahead, her passivity appalls her. She had given in, yielded to browbeating. Paralyzed by grief, she hadn't even tried to explain about the disastrous weekend in Newport with Nick. Ellen would have understood, and proposed a weekend in New York or Montreal instead. But Alice would have grilled her and wondered why she hadn't told them long ago.

Liz watches Nick, sleeping quietly beside her. In the morning light, the scar over his right eyebrow is a tiny pool of shadow. Lying on his back, he is calm in his dreams. She slows her breathing to match his. Reflections of light from the water dapple the ceiling. The room is small, the carpet threadbare. But there's a small balcony and the harbor just below is mostly empty, quiet in April.

She gingerly touches her belly, flat and taut for now. Is this how three months pregnant feels? She can't detect any change. But she knows; other symptoms are clear. How to tell him? Had they still been just friends, she believes she could have told him; he would have listened and helped her decide what to do. Now, she is uncertain, fearful he'll withdraw from her or reject her.

He begins to wake, rolling over to face her, blue eyes reflecting the low light dappling the ceiling.

"Well?"

"Good morning," she says, touching his face. For her, it had been love at first sight. It had taken him most of a year to find his way through their friendship to love. She hadn't minded. She loved him, after all. And then, the shock of his body, his skin against her; they had been desperate to make up for lost time. And so they do now, moving together on this April morning, finding each other.

Alice is driving. Occasionally, she glances at Liz. Her eyes, in the rearview mirror, questioning. Liz tries not to notice. She leans back and turns to watch the passing fields. The landscape in this part of Connecticut, just before the Rhode Island border, reminds her of Burgundy's rolling hills. During her last trip to France with Scott, before they knew how sick he was, they had stayed in a village where a tiny Romanesque church had been turned into a garden shed. Scott, a preservationist, was bemused. But Liz, an architectural historian, knew this wasn't unusual in a region where Romanesque ruins outnumber vineyards. Here in Connecticut, the farmland is disused, barns abandoned, awaiting the next incursion of developers. Little hope that any existing structure stands a chance against them. How many hours had she spent listening to Scott rail against the waste?

Liz closes her eyes, listening to Alice and Ellen talking, their voices barely above a murmur. Leaning her head against the window, she feels again the numbness that came over her that morning, and her fear of Nick's reaction to what she had to tell him, her doubt about what to do. Today, travelling to Newport for the first time in 30 years, she is cocooned in her friends' concern for her grief, relieved that's all they know.

Seagulls dive; ducks and geese paddle among the fishing boats. After breakfast that day, they stroll on the Cliff Walk, its surf-slicked path treacherous underfoot. As usual, Nick is talking plants—botany, his "true love," according to their friends. Liz knows better.

The beech trees, their branches outlined in pink against the dark grey bark, show leaves beginning to lose their casings. The contrast in proportions—delicate leaves and massive trunks—makes them smile: "Like hippos in tutus..." Nick laughs. Along the Walk, the wild roses, laden with last year's hips, look more dead than alive after a winter of wind and salt spray. But Liz imagines June, the roses in bloom, a rose-infused fog blanketing the cliff.

Nick is quiet; Liz accepts, rehearsing silently what she will say and how she will explain what she knows she must do. Surely he will agree? There isn't any way that having this baby makes sense, given everything. Meaning: Given Nick's plans. We can have babies later. You know that. I've made the appointment. Please accept this. Please.

She sighs. Nick turns to her, his eyes, questioning. She takes his hand. They both start to speak. Hearing the intensity in Nick's voice, Liz stops. She pulls him to a bench overlooking the water, listening.

Liz knows that Alice believes she isn't managing her life very well. Alice is always full of advice drawn from articles she has read about every imaginable problem and self-help books that hold out promises of a more fulfilling life—if one simply eats better, or less, gets more sleep or exercise—or one of the many personal improvement workshops she attends. She's a successful lawyer, not because of the advice she gleans from these many sources, but because she is smart and, by nature, compulsively well-organized and motivated. That she herself has failed at marriage, doesn't stop Alice from advising her friends about theirs. Liz understands that her advice is an expression of caring. She listens, but seldom acts on it.

After Scott's funeral, Alice had proposed that Liz take a cruise, "because it would be a good change of pace and you need rest." Somewhere she had read about someone who had taken a trip around the world after her husband died and had found it salutary. When Liz demurred, Alice claimed she was "indulging" her grief. There's more truth to this than she knows.

"There's something I've never told anyone. Something I want you to know, before..." Nick's eyes widen, his mouth tightens.

"OK, it's OK," she says. "Tell me."

Nick talks slowly, effortfully, as though reliving the events. He was ten at the time; his brother, Scott, twelve. They were at a summer camp on Lake Champlain. Scott excelled at sports. Nick did not. Time after time, Scott had tried to coach him, to no avail. At last, Scott left him alone.

Nick pauses, swallowing hard. "I was jealous of Scott, so jealous. I wanted so much to be like him." Their parents had basked in the glow of Scott's triumphs, oblivious to Nick's quieter successes. When he was nine or ten, Nick began to hope that Scott would fail at something, anything at all. When Scott was up at bat, Nick wished for him to strike out. When he swam in a race, Nick willed him to miss his turn.

"One Sunday afternoon that summer at camp, I was out on a point overlooking the lake. There was no one around." Nick looks at her then. "I was breaking a rule by being out on my own, but I didn't expect anyone to see me, because everyone else was at lunch."

He had stopped for a while to sit in the lee of a boulder. There was a good breeze blowing off the lake. Warmed by the sun, he fell asleep, waking to the sound of thunder and raindrops on his face.

Just as it began to rain hard, the wind hit him full force. He looked out on the lake and recognized Scott, alone in a sailboat, struggling to lower the mainsail to ride out the storm. Nick could see that the sail was stuck. He knew that unless Scott could release it, the boat would *capsize. Scott was now on the far side of the point from the camp; no one could see him. Transfixed by Scott's efforts, Nick remained motionless. Then, in a violent gust of wind, the boat capsized. Scott disappeared in the water.*

Nick ran back in the rain to his cabin. Jack and Bob, two of his cabin mates, were playing cards. They stopped long enough to rag him about getting caught in the rain, but soon left him alone. Nick stripped, climbed shivering into his bunk, and fell asleep.

As Nick learned later, a lifeguard had spotted Scott spread-eagled across the boat's hull, adrift in the choppy lake. With another counselor, he went after Scott in one of the ski boats. Scott hadn't been wearing a life vest or a safety line. It was sheer luck he hadn't gone under, that he hadn't drowned.

By the time their parents arrived the next day, summoned by the camp director, Scott had become the camp hero. Nick stayed in his cabin, steering clear of the hubbub. He knew it was too late to tell anyone of his failure to act. And if he did tell someone, how would he explain why he hadn't run for help? After the accident Nick went to every ball game, tennis match, and swim meet, cheering Scott on with his whole heart trying to drown his shame.

Nick tells Liz, "Nothing helps. I can't forget sitting there that day watching him fight that sail, doing nothing." Nick is asking for forgiveness. Liz knows he needs to forgive himself, first. For now, she holds him tight.

"Later," she thinks. "I'll tell him later."

When they reach their turnpike exit, Alice says, "I'm going to stop up here at the nearest gas station. I'm almost out." Ellen grins back at Liz. Alice knows the route well; there are few gas stations along the country roads.

Liz remembers another trip to France with Scott. She had been driving their rental car. Making a tight turn into a narrow street, she had misjudged the distance and knocked off the side mirror of a car parked near the corner. Because she spoke French and Scott didn't, it fell to her to figure out what to do. Although the gendarme continued to address Scott, it was Liz who answered the questions and filled out the paperwork once the owner of the damaged car appeared. Scott had taken this in stride, had been amused by it, in fact. He had shown tact and good humor. How she misses his even temper, his understanding of how and when to defer, qualities that had made him an outstanding negotiator.

Liz answers the phone on the first ring, eyes the clock—two hours since Nick had dropped her off. He was checking in.

"Good timing!" she says. "I'm almost..."

"Drunk driver...Oh, God, Liz, drunk driver. He's..." Liz is confused. What drunk driver? Then, stunned. As the phone slips out of her hand, she hears Nick's roommate, Jack, "...gone. Liz? Lizzie? Are you there?...OK?"

Wakeful that night, she hears Jack's voice repeating, "Drunk driver, oh, God, Liz, drunk driver... He's gone." Ellen holding her, Alice offering her car. Late the next morning, she reaches Nick's parents.

They are staying in Nick and Jack's apartment and urge her to meet them.

As she drives north that day, memories of Nick come to her in fragments. Only 24 hours ago, she thinks, only 24 hours ago we were having breakfast in Newport. She hears his voice, sees his smile, feels the shape and warmth of his hand in hers. Yesterday...

One day, watching him sketch, she noticed his expression change as he started and finished each part. His eyes got darker as he worked. At first alert and eager, eyes rapidly sweeping the paper, eventually he fixed more and more on the drawing itself, appraising it, weighing its features, until he put the pencil down. Nick had loved to draw, almost as much as he had loved plants. She blinks tears away, forcing herself to focus on the road.

Abdominal pain hits her suddenly; waves of it. What had begun that morning as a dull ache has become a knife, rhythmically thrusting into her. Involuntarily, she begins to pant. She pulls over at the next rest stop, gets out of the car. The dark wet stain on the seat is slick to the touch. "Oh, no ..." Doubled over, she grabs her overnight bag and makes her way unsteadily to the restroom. For a moment, she floats above herself in the stall, seeing her blood draining away in rivulets down her thighs, as though this were someone else's miscarriage. She staunches the bleeding with toilet paper, then a pad, washes, changes, and returns to the car. She watches herself drive out of the rest area, the remainder of the trip a blank.

Alice and Ellen have always wondered about Liz and Scott's decision not to have children. But neither has pressed her for more of an explanation than the one she originally gave: Each committed to a demanding profession—her teaching and writing, his litigation—neither comfortable with the idea of a nanny, they had decided to forgo a family. Liz's miscarriage—which she had kept from Scott and her two friends—was the probable cause. Only Liz's doctor knew her history and respected her decision not to tell Scott.

At Nick's memorial service, friends and family sit in the cool, dark chapel. Liz has brought a letter, written to him in the days after the crash. His mother, Louisa, a pianist, has selected the music, piano pieces she and Nick loved. The service is less formal, with fewer prayers than Liz had expected. Seated between Ellen and Alice, she relaxes against the pew to listen to the testimonials.

Scott speaks first. Liz has met him only once before, at the end of his first Vietnam tour. So, when she hears his voice, it shocks her. He sounds so much like Nick. She closes her eyes and listens.

"When Nick and I were in high school, I went with him one day on one of his walks. Everyone who knew Nick knows how much he liked to walk. Everyone knows how much he objected to calling these walks hikes. As he so often said, he wasn't walking to anywhere; he was walking for the sake of looking." Scott smiles. "And look he did.

At anything green and growing. No plant was too small, no flower too insignificant.

"He'd bring out his magnifying glass and hunker down next to something that looked for all the world like just another weed and spend a good amount of time taking notes—or talking—about this plant and its peculiarities.

"On this walk I'm talking about, Nick was looking for something special. I don't remember now what it was, but he knew exactly what he hoped to find. Most of you know that walking with Nick when he was looking hard for something involved more stopping than walking. I was used to this, but I was feeling a bit restless, and occasionally wandered off when he stopped to look at something.

"At first, he tolerated my wandering. Then he got kind of annoyed and asked me to stay put. When I pointed out to him that my staying put shouldn't matter to him, since he was focusing on his search, he told me that for him to be able to look properly I had to be still so as not to distract him. When I protested, he said, 'Look, Scott, when you're pitching, don't you want people to be quiet?' He was right about that. As any pitcher knows, focus is essential.

"When I agreed with him about this, he said, 'OK. When I'm looking at a plant, I need quiet so that I don't miss anything. If I'm distracted, I may get it wrong. Here. Let me show you something.' He picked two leaves, each from a different plant. To me, they looked the same. Then he pulled out his magnifying glass and showed me the two leaves, side by side. Both had serrated edges, but one of them had small filaments on its underside. These were invisible to the naked eye. 'It's easier for me to see this kind of thing if I'm not wondering

where you've gone, OK?' From then on, whenever he stopped to look at something, I stood by, waiting for him to be ready to move on.

"From this experience, I learned to restrain my fidgeting. Also, I learned to slow down. Although he never learned to play tennis with me, the times we spent together on the trail are among the most precious times I've spent with anyone. Nick, wherever you are, please know that I'm walking more and hiking less."

Several people are nodding and smiling. When Liz opens her eyes, she sees Nick's parents, Bill's arm around Louisa, her head bent forward into her hands. Scott folds his notes, then sits beside his mother, his arm reaching around her to clasp his father's shoulder.

As he is leaving, Scott approaches her. "Do you have a minute?"

"Yes, of course. Let me just tell Ellen and Alice I'll catch up with them." She comes back to find Scott sitting on a couch in an alcove off the entryway. She sits beside him. For a moment, he looks at her.

"In some ways," he says, "Nick's death must have been an even greater shock to you than it was to us." When she begins to protest, he shakes his head. "I suppose you must know that Nick wrote me many long letters when I was in 'Nam. And his letters were full of you. It was obvious he loved you very much. I am so sorry." She smiles through her tears.

"Stay in touch, OK?"

"Yes," she nods. "That would mean a lot. Thank you."

Liz lived at home during the next year, sticking with her plan to do graduate work in art history. There were days when she felt normal. But much of the time, she had a sensation of being suspended somewhere between the past and the present, never fully in one or the other.

On the phone one day with Ellen, she said, "I still find myself thinking that he's just away for a while, and that when he gets back, life will go on." When Ellen didn't say anything, Liz added, "That our life together will go on, I mean." Then Ellen said, "I know, Liz, but, you've got to face it, your life *is* going on. And that's got to be enough for now, don't you think?" Liz gave a short laugh. "Maybe. But I don't have to like it."

"No, you don't. You must keep going as best you can."

Liz began to edit her conversations with Ellen and Alice, telling them only about what she was doing in her classes, and brushing aside their efforts to get her to talk about how she was "really."

Toward the end of October, she calls the Dunnings. Louisa picks up. "Liz! How wonderful to hear from you. Where are you? Can you stop by?"

"I'd love to come by, but actually I'm at home now."

"You know, Liz, we'd really love to see you. Would you like to come up for Thanksgiving? Could you do that? That way we could have a good long visit. Scott will be here, but it will just be the three of us—unless you join us, of course." For a moment, Liz can't speak, can't get beyond the lump in her throat.

"Of course, you may have other plans. If not, please do come. Really, we'd love to have you." Liz closes without committing herself, promising only to check back. She knows her parents will be away in November. The trouble is, she doesn't know if she is ready to be with Nick's family without Nick.

One evening in September, the phone rang. At the sound of the familiar voice, she couldn't speak. Scott, hearing her confusion, gave her an immediate out, "Have I caught you at a bad time, Liz? Shall I call back?"

"No, it's fine. This is a good time. I need a break from barrel vaults. They all look alike!"

Scott laughed with her.

"Now that we've sorted that out ... Mom asked me to check in with you about Thanksgiving. She told me that you might have felt a bit pressured to say 'yes' to her. She's hoping that I can add a little persuasive power to the pressure, so that you'll agree to keep us company. What do you think?"

Liz felt comforted and calmed. Scott might have sounded like Nick, but he had a different sense of humor. Nick would never have laughed with her about barrel vaults, any more than she would have joked with him about plant classification. To Nick, systems of any kind were no joking matter.

"I'd like that. I'm sorry I haven't called."

"You know, it might help my parents to have you here. If that makes it any easier for you to come up." She grabbed this life preserver. He seemed to have a knack for it.

"That's a good thought. I'll keep it in mind, thanks. Tell me about you, Scott. How are you?"

His voice drops. "I'm doing OK, I guess. I've been helping my father a bit in his business and thinking about what I'll do next, probably law school. For now, just getting back in the swing of things is challenge enough." He laughs. "I'll tell you more when I see you."

For the first time in several months, Liz no longer feels like the missing piece of a jigsaw puzzle.

The first anniversary of Nick's death, Liz had spent the weekend with the Dunnings, helping in the garden, cooking with Louisa. Late that Saturday night, after his parents had gone to bed, Scott had sat with Liz in their living room looking through photo albums. There had been images of Nick, most of them showing him peering into a microscope or assembling some project or other.

Many of the photos of Scott spotlighted his athletic successes. In nearly every one of them, it seemed, he held a trophy, surrounded by jubilant team members. In one he sat on a camp cot in a room that looked like an infirmary, his face swollen and visibly bruised.

"What about this one?"

He chuckled. "Long story made short?" he asked. Liz nodded.

"I was in a sailing accident at camp. Almost drowned. Got knocked around when the boat capsized. I wasn't wearing a life jacket. Very close call. Somehow, I survived. But, boy, did I get in a lot of trouble." He glanced at Liz, then went on.

"I was twelve at the time. And I was a pretty good sailor. Still, I needed permission to take the boat out on my own. That day, I didn't even sign the boat out, so no one knew where it was, let alone that I had it. This was on Lake Champlain, where sailing a small boat under the best of circumstances is very tricky—the breeze is fluky as hell, especially in August when big storm systems move through.

"A major thunderstorm blew up. I probably would have been OK if I'd been able to get the sail down. But it got stuck and nothing I did made any difference. A big gust blew the boat over and I went overboard—no life vest, no tether. Luckily, just as I went over, I saw someone running through the woods toward camp. I guessed whoever it was must have gone for help. I hung onto the boat until they came for me."

Until this moment, Liz hadn't realized she had been holding her breath. Now she let it out in a rush. It was Nick, and of course Scott hadn't recognized him.

"I woke up lying face down on the hull, one of the sheets wrapped around me. Next thing I know, Sammy, the head lifeguard, is next to me. Jake the tennis coach steered a ski-boat next to us. They got me off the boat and into the ski-boat and wrapped me in a bunch of towels and blankets. I was pretty bruised, but I was OK." Scott glanced at her. "That is, until my dad got there the next day. He gave me the worst bawling out I've ever gotten, told me I was old enough to know better than to go out on my own in a boat without telling anyone, and grounded me for the rest of the summer. That hurt more than my bruises.

"Sometimes I even think that the powers that be arranged things just so I'd learn my lesson early. Until that day, I took all kinds of risks, never thinking ahead to the consequences. That accident taught me to think things through." Smiling, Scott looked at Liz and said, "Now, I always make sure the equipment is in good working order." Then, "And I always sign the boat out and wear my life jacket!" They both laughed.

Lying in bed that night, unable to sleep, Liz thinks about the two versions of the sailing crisis. Nick had held himself responsible for Scott's accident; Scott had seen him—without recognizing him, true—running away, and thought he was running for help. Staring into the darkness, she feels something inside her give way, like a knot coming undone, releasing feelings that had been pent up for a year. Tears, then. Grief for Nick merges with her sorrow that he and Scott had never had the chance to talk about that day on the lake, or to hear Scott laugh about what, to him, had been just one of life's lessons.

Should she tell Scott Nick's secret? If she does, she will no longer bear the burden of Nick's shame alone. If not, she will spare him the knowledge that Nick had witnessed the accident and done nothing to help him.

Telling Scott will only hurt and confuse him. Not telling him will protect both him and Nick, preserving intact Scott's memory of his brother and the self-knowledge he gained that day on the lake. Keeping a secret is not the same thing as telling a lie. Of this she is confident. In not revealing what she knows, she is honoring her love for Nick. Perhaps, in time, knowing that she was doing right would come to feel right to her.

Later she realized this was the first sign she was falling in love with Scott.

Early in her marriage to Scott, Liz sometimes wondered what would have happened had Nick survived and told Scott about that afternoon on the lake. Over time, as she learned to love Scott, she understood just how much Scott had admired and respected Nick. It became clear to her that Scott had valued Nick for all the ways he was different from himself and that he had longed to be more like him. In the beginning, he would have forgiven Nick, because he was a generous, compassionate man. In time, he would have given Nick what he needed most, his understanding. Perhaps, eventually, they would have laughed about it.

From the back seat, looking ahead, Liz can see the Newport Bridge. Through a light fog, the noon sun casts a golden haze over its two towers. She catches and holds Alice's eyes in the rearview mirror.

In the passenger seat, Ellen turns around to face her, "OK?" she asks.

"Mm-hm," Liz answers. She leans forward to touch Ellen's shoulder. "Thanks."

When Liz next looks out the car window, the quality of light has changed. Overhead, like pebbles on a beach, bright patches of blue sky are strewn amid the dispersing fog. Bridge traffic is inching along as weekenders take the off-ramp toward the center of town. She opens her window, inhales deeply, drawing in the salt air. In the back of her throat she senses its bitter tang, its hint of rose.

It is as though she were absorbing the essences of ocean and rose. Closing her eyes, she watches a wave receding from the shore, a sailboat bobbing on the horizon.

Moving Day

When Ann meets the movers to sign the paperwork, the driver reminds her about the hurricane that is expected to reach the south coast of Connecticut that afternoon. "We should be in Pittsburgh by late morning tomorrow." He shakes his head. "Floyd, they named it. Lucky for us, he's headed northeast. Not so lucky for you, I guess." He smiles. "California, here we come. See you next month."

After the moving van leaves, she carries her sleeping bag and backpack upstairs to the front bedroom. Driving down together from Boston, Evan, Lauren, and Zoe would arrive in time for dinner at the Rhumb Line. When Ann had proposed that they bring their sleeping bags, that they spend the night in the house together, they had agreed right away. Zoe had called back. "I want to see the house again, before someone buys it. It's still ours." Her voice caught. "And Dad? All my memories of him there are still so clear. I can still hear his voice, Ann." Ann knows. She can still hear Steven's voice, too, the way he cleared his throat, the way he said certain common things like, "You're too much, sweetie, you know?" dragging out "too," lifting it with his smile, his love.

Evan and Zoe are both working full time in Boston now. Lauren had found a summer job and is sharing an apartment with Zoe until she goes back to college for her senior year. They have planned to leave around 4:30, Zoe had told her. "But don't worry if we don't get there before six," she had cautioned. "You know the traffic." Ann doesn't have a plan, exactly, just a vague but urgent desire to visit and say goodbye to the house. She hopes this will stir her memories of her life there with Steven, before he got sick, before he died.

"The death of a loved one challenges you in so many ways." Ann's best friend, Joan, a psychiatrist and grief counselor, had told her. Joan advised her to take her time, to keep a notebook with her and write down her memories, no matter how random or insignificant they might seem. "Spend some time alone in the house, spend the night, if you can. Remembering Steven there with you may bring up events, stories, even disagreements. Make notes, of course, because someday, you may want to tell the story, your story and his."

Ann spreads her sleeping bag on the floor and sits on it, leaning against the wall. Closing her eyes, she sees the room again as it had been before the movers began to empty the house: the cherry dresser, the twin beds, the night table with the chipped glass top, the botanical prints hanging on the walls, the cherry-framed mirror over the fireplace. Stripped bare, the room asserts its original personality: plain and simple. Also, it reveals its age—the uneven plaster walls, the warped floorboards, the bowed ceiling. Like every other room in the house except the kitchen, which is only 75 years old, this one wears its age with quiet pride.

Once, early on, a visiting friend from California had asked if they had considered gutting the interior, replacing the floorboards and insulating the walls, installing and sealing aluminum storm windows. "Just think how much you'll save on heating, Ann." Steven had caught Ann's eye with a slight warning headshake. "Great idea, Joan. We'll think about it," Ann had replied.

Of course, they had worked on the house—painting and restoring walls and floorboards. And they had installed new storm windows and blown in insulation. But they left untouched the sagging ceiling and the warped floorboards. The character of the house remained intact.

Would Floyd blow out to sea or make his way up the coast to Rhode Island and Massachusetts? She puts her portable radio on the floor beside her, tunes it in, and catches the end of the weather report. "...on track to reach Rhode Island this evening,.." Fortunately, she had made an early dinner reservation at the Rhumb Line. They would all be tucked in, out of harm's way, by eight o'clock.

Then, she goes through the downstairs, room by room, checking drawers, cupboards, and closets. Her search yields one comic book (20 years old), an ancient pack of Beechnut gum, two marbles, and a comb. In the master bathroom cabinet, she discovers the velvet pouch she'd bought years ago. In it, her mother's long lost pearl earrings, loaned to her for the wedding. How had the pouch ended up here? Her mother had refused the replacement pair Ann offered, remorseful. "You keep them, sweetie, and if ever the others turn up, you can return them." The damper in the kitchen fireplace slams shut as it often did in windstorms. She closes her eyes, listening. Yes, the wind is rising. In any windstorm, gusts often swooped down the two chimneys, moaning, squealing, rattling the dampers. The three kids had loved the racket, especially Evan, who developed a repertoire of whooshes, hoots, and bellows, which he belted out, as if challenging the wind to do him one better.

The kitchen fireplace and chimney were 75 years old. Rarely used, because it drew poorly, the walk-in fireplace had been built by someone who hadn't considered the prevailing winds. During their first big storm, just after they moved in, they lit a small fire. For a while, it burned fine. Then, the nor'easter landed, seemingly right on top of them. As the wind huffed and puffed, the smoke billowed into the kitchen and on into the first floor and up the stairs. There was no door between the kitchen and the dining room. Steven had used their fire extinguisher to put it out.

On the other hand, the original central chimney, which serviced four fireplaces, worked fine. For three hundred years, retaining the heat created by the fires laid and tended in all four fireplaces, this warm core heated the keeping room, the sitting room, and the two upstairs bedrooms. Sometimes, waking early on a winter morning, Ann imagined how it must have been, living in the house in the

1800s, sheltered from winter storms, basking in the warmth. She wondered how many cords were needed to get through the winter. She imagined tending the fires throughout the day, banking them at night, reviving them in the morning.

Sometimes she felt as if she knew the families that had occupied the house, most of them descendants of the original owner, He likely had been a ship's carpenter, a Quaker, who had built the house himself. She arrived at this idea based on the built-in storage areas such as the beehive-shaped "drying room" constructed within the old chimney, and on the height of the doorways: Only someone accustomed to ducking through a ship's narrow passageways would have been comfortable with the limited six-foot clearances of the doorways. Steven, just six-feet tall, didn't notice until Ann pointed it out. Evan, now six-feet-two had to adjust every time he visited.

As Ann and Steven soon discovered, owning an eighteenth-century house in Newport's historic district was all the introduction they needed. Neighbors stopped to introduce themselves and to pass along the names of handymen skilled in the care and repair of old houses, sharing details about the history and development of the area, and, of course, the stories of their own houses. Intrigued that Steven was a native Californian, they had teased him: "What'll you do when it snows?"

During his last illness, his last winter, Steven lay still, looking out at the falling snow, as Ann read to him. Once, he said, "I've always loved the snow."

"Always?"

"I spent my junior year in Chambéry, remember? Sometimes, we went over to Aix-les-Bains, to ski. Most of the time on those days, I sat in the café, watching the snow swirl down and around the ski slope, thinking about how each snowflake is different. Just imagine that."

Filtered through the thickening cloud cover, the sunlight layers wan swathes on the floors and the plaster walls, dimpled here and there by the holes left by picture hooks. When the wind subsides momentarily, Ann hears a low hum, like the sound the furnace made just before it clicked on. But it's the middle of September, and the furnace has been off for several months. Had the house inspector turned it on, then left without turning it off?

She opens the pantry door, which faces the refrigerator. The door is ajar. Unplugged.

Perhaps the sound she hears is coming from an idling car. Upstairs she crosses the front bedroom, off the hallway, and opens one of the windows. From there she can see the intersection, which is empty. Not an idling car. Leaves swirl down the streaming gutters to the storm drains at the corner. Behind the house across the street, a sycamore maple sways, its wide canopy arching, catching, then moving back and away. The picket fence wobbles at the corner of the driveway. To the right of the driveway, the telephone pole judders. The wires rise and fall, Ann leans out the window.

The hum is coming from the transformer bolted to the top of the pole. Ann slides down to sit on the floor under the window as the wind rises, sweeping in from the southeast, from the past.

When Ann and Steven moved to Newport in July 1985, neighbors advised them to stock up on candles and flashlight batteries, canned food and cornflakes. Neither of them had experienced a hurricane, but the neighbors assured them these preparations were necessary. "In hurricane season—I mean, now, of course—you never know. We may even have to evacuate," an older neighbor told them. "We'll have plenty of warning, don't you worry," she'd added.

"Abandon the house? Then what? Where will we go?"

Steven shrugged. "We'll probably see some heavy rain and wind, a big storm, but nothing that's going to drive us out." Ann didn't argue. Instead, she bought more candles and flashlight batteries.

Two weeks later, soon after she and Steven went to bed, the wind began to pummel the house, shaking the shutters, whistling down the chimneys. Neither of them had been able to sleep. At 3 o'clock, there was a lull, the air heavy and still. Ann held her breath, waiting. Then, in a burst of rain and hail, the howling began. They held hands and lay still, feeling the house shudder as the wind lashed it. Both chimneys growled and moaned.

Two candles, one on each of the night tables, flickered in the draft that crept in around the fireplace damper.

During another lull at 4:30, they heard a loud crackle and a single crash of thunder. "Lightning strike, a close one," Steven said, getting out of bed. From the front bedroom, he called, "The pole across the street is down, the transformer's sparking."

"Is the pole on fire?" Ann stood at the second window.

"Can't tell from here. And I don't want to go out to see what's going on. I'm going to call."

Ann followed him downstairs. He held the kitchen phone to his ear, hung it up. "Dead."

Sirens shrilled in the distance. If the pole caught fire, would emergency workers arrive before the flames reached the house?

"Let's keep an eye on it. If necessary, I'll turn on the hose. Standing at the front gate, I should be able to reach it." Steven's grin gleamed in the candlelight. They both laughed at the idea of putting out a fire in a rainstorm.

She hugged him. "I'll bet this house has seen plenty of hurricanes." The house was two hundred and fifty years old. "Like barnacles, it's a survivor."

Just then, flashing lights zig-zagged across the ceiling. Airbrakes hissed. A truck door slammed. The front gate opened; the wind slammed it shut. A man called, "Anybody home?"

On the steps, a fireman in a yellow storm jacket removed his hat. "We're spraying fire foam on that pole, sir." He pointed his hat at the street. "The electric company crew will be here soon. They'll take care of the transformer."

He settled his hat back on his head and snugged the brim down. "It's nearly five now. The storm should be out of here by mid-afternoon at the latest."

"Any idea when we'll have power?" Steven asked.

"Your guess is as good as mine. First, we have to make sure it's safe to start it up again. Best thing to do now? Put on some warm clothes, keep your candles going, stay inside and dry, and stand by."

Later, they learned there were trees and power lines down all over the island, boats torn from their moorings and tossed on top of one another against the pilings. Sparks from snapped power lines had caused fires in several places.

Throughout the day, sirens shrieked as emergency crews raced to stem the damage.

That week the local paper covered the storm damage. Newport had been spared the worst of it. Thanks to the wind shift that occurred in the early morning, the hurricane had turned away from the coast, inland, where it quickly weakened. A few boats in Newport Harbor had been blown up on the docks, but most had remained unscathed and the emergency crews had quickly cleared fallen trees and righted or replaced electrical poles. Gathering in local coffee shops, long-term residents regaled one another with stories of previous—and worse—storms.

"Our first hurricane," Ann said. "I think we passed Storm Survival, Part 1, don't you? I suppose Part 2 will cover blizzards."

"At least we now know a little better what to expect." Steven smiled. "Except, of course, we'll have to add firewood to our list of emergency supplies."

"Don't forget down comforters and slippers."

During their twenty-five years in the house, they had survived hurricanes, ice-storms, and blizzards. It was the domestic storms, during their first ten years together, which left them depleted and uncertain, both torn by conflicting motives and objectives, facing one another across widening gulfs of misunderstanding.

After Ann and Steven married, after their first year together in Santa Cruz, Steven had applied for the teaching job in Newport. Ann, a travel writer, often joked about her portable job—"You *can* take it with you," Steven assured her—and looked forward to being closer to New York and Boston. She could leave the car at the station in Kingston and take the train. "I'll be the first kid on the block to have an office with a moving view," Ann told her friends.

At the end of the week Steven spent visiting the school, while Ann met with a realtor, she and Steven had gone through the house Ann had put at the top of her list of four possibilities. Ann was enchanted. Three hundred years old, on the National Historic Register, it had been restored. The beamed ceilings and crown moldings, the wide-board floors, the uneven texture of the horsehair plaster walls—all hallmarks of the 18th-century house she had known as a child and adolescent—welcomed Ann back to a world she knew and loved.

She felt comfortable taking charge of an antique house. She knew how to repair cracks in plaster walls, how to sand and varnish wood floors, expected—and enjoyed—the uneven floorboards. Born and raised in Bennington, Vermont, 250 miles north and inland, Ann told Steven that Newport felt like a long-lost cousin.

She kept her misgivings to herself: Accustomed to the ranch house in Santa Cruz, how would they adjust to living in this antique, which required TLC—no stomping, slamming, or rough-housing, except, of course, outdoors. That's what Ann thought would save them: Living near the harbor and the beach, where they could swim every day or take sailing lessons, would that trade-off satisfy them? Would they accommodate? She hoped that sharing the history of this area—this house—they'd eventually feel the same way about it as she had felt about her own childhood home.

"Sister Ann," Steven sometimes teased, on account of her preference for Shaker and Quaker traditions. It amused her to think that in an earlier life, she might have lived among the practitioners of the simple faith in a house like this one.

Enthusiastic about the house, about making a fresh start together, they had been such optimists, she and Steven. She had believed love conquers all, had believed she could have it all, and figure out her role in the children's lives by putting her mind to it.

She believed she could win them over. How quickly the obstacles proved her wrong.

The dining room, the house's original keeping room, catches and holds the light reflected from the house next door and the shadow play from the dogwood and star magnolia in the garden across the lawn. This is the heart of the house, its largest public room. One must pass through it to get to the kitchen, an addition built in the twenties.

Due to its size, shape, and function—it was the original kitchen, designed for casual, workaday encounters—they had furnished it simply with a small sofa and several side chairs. Ann wanted it to be a space where they could come together, face to face as a family during the children's summer visits. The living room was too formal, the kitchen too small. Much later, she and Steven realized what the house lacked: What Ann called "cozy corners," spaces the children could call their own. They had never felt at home here, she knows.

When the children arrived for their first summer visit, they had been awestruck by the eight-by-ten-foot cistern, which lay beneath the dining room. Annually, they learned, it filled and drained with fresh water, although it never overflowed. In the seventh grade, Evan called it a waystation on the underground railroad in an essay he wrote about the Civil War.

"Molly wants me to talk to him," Steven told Ann. "He needs to know he can't make up stuff like this."

"How do you know it isn't true, Dad?" Evan demanded when they spoke on the phone. "There's room enough down there for a couple of people."

"I also know it's usually half full of water. You've helped me pump it out, remember? How could anyone hide down there without getting very wet and very cold? And sick."

"Well, just suppose the people came when the cistern was empty, like in the summer."

"Maybe. Still, there's no evidence. You could have said in your paper that runaway slaves *might* have hidden in our cistern. '*Might have hidden*' is a far cry from 'did hide.' I bet your teacher would accept your paper if you wrote it that way."

"You mean I should ask her?"

"Yes. And let me know what she says, OK?"

Evan's teacher allowed him to revise his paper and told Molly she was impressed he was so optimistic, convinced that many Newport residents at the time wanted to help the slaves, to keep them safe on their perilous journey.

For twenty-two years, the house had sheltered them from hurricanes, blizzards, and other upheavals—Ann's breast cancer,

Steven's struggles with the politics of managing his department at the school, the children's growing pains.

As she prepared now to return to California, Ann understood one thing: the house had provided them shelter, but it was, in the end, a temporary one. When she compared how she felt about it with the way she had felt about her childhood home, she realized that she had never felt "at home" here, as if the house were a second skin, that it was a place where she could confidently withdraw from the world, safe and secure, at least for the time it might take to recover, to heal, before moving on.

Leaving the house means casting off her years of becoming a middle-aged adult, the entire process, the fits and starts, the depths and heights, the comedies, melodramas, and tragedies. It means leaving her years with Steven behind, every large and small adjustment each had made to the other, the unresolved hurts, the glow of their pleasure in each other's company. "A new day," she thinks.

The shadows are deepening now, filling the house's empty corners, blurring its imperfections. Like the house, she has been smoothed by her own aging, which has softened most of her hard edges, prepared her to move on.

Two years ago, before he died, she had promised Steven she would wait at least two years before making any plans. He had reminded her then, with amusement, of his decision to buy the house he had lived in before he met her, just after his divorce from Molly. "I was desperate to have a place of my own for the kids on the weekends," he said. "So desperate, I never bothered to have the house inspected, or, believe me, I would never have bought it."

As it had turned out, a construction flaw in the chimney had required extensive and costly repairs, which Steven, paying alimony and child support, could ill afford. "I should have taken more time. And so should you. Promise me, Ann?" At that moment, Ann thought about how they always had made decisions together, even this one. "Sure, sweetie." Unable then to imagine him gone, she made this promise, as if making it would prolong his life.

Now adults, the children, of course, had other ideas.

Evan urged her to keep the house, to rent it, and take out a home equity loan to purchase the condo she was moving to in Monterey. Even after Ann had a buyer under contract, Lauren had tried to persuade Evan and Zoe to combine their resources with hers, to buy the house so that they all could use it.

The sale is now a fait accompli. Ann will meet the three of them for dinner at the Rhumb Line in an hour. Until then, she will take the time to revisit her memories and to say goodbye.

Downstairs once again, she removes the beach towel from her satchel, spreads it in the middle of the keeping room floor, lies down on her back, hands folded, legs stretched out, relaxed, and closes her eyes.

It was 4 o'clock. The wind had picked up again. Evan, Lauren, and Zoe expected her to meet them for dinner at 6:30 at the Rhumb Line. They were driving down together from Boston. Most likely they were already on the road. Too late to cancel. Ann was staying at a local B&B. They might have to spend the night there, too. This morning, as Ann was leaving, the proprietor had said she'd had several cancellations. She'd be happy to have three additional overnight guests

She understands the children's desire to keep the house, one way or another. All three are still coming to terms with Steven's death. Whenever they get together, they tell their stories about him, in the present tense, as if they had just visited him: "Dad always says …" "Dad thinks we should …" It was as if by parroting his opinions, they could bring him back.

And Ann's memories? In the early days with the children, their summers in Newport, she could do nothing right. Zoe spoke to her in monosyllables. Lauren demanded explanations: "Why do I have to make my bed every morning?" Angry at Steven and Molly, Evan blamed Ann for the divorce. Ann schooled herself not to fight back.

Evan slurps his milk.

"Cut it out!" Lauren pushes back from the table, slamming her chair against the wall. Another dent in the woodwork. Across the kitchen at the sink, Ann cringes.

She rinses out the coffee pot, sets it in the dish rack and turns around. "It's time to get ready, kids," she says.

Evan burps. "Ready for what?"

Lauren rolls her eyes.

"Sailing. Your class starts at nine, remember?" Ann tells him. Of course, he remembers. He likes the class. But he also likes taunting her. She dries her hands, folds the towel, and hangs it up. It's nearly 8:30. "Ten minutes. Our deal, remember?"

"Your deal, you mean." He tilts his chair back, balancing on two legs, releases his grip on the table just long enough to begin to wobble. Ann ignores him.

On her way out of the kitchen, Lauren mutters, "Just do it, would you? And hurry up. We were late last time."

The chair bangs down. Evan drops his napkin on the table and gulps the rest of his orange juice.

Although Molly had initiated the divorce, she blamed Steven. Living with her, the kids heard nothing but criticisms of Steven, and witnessed or overheard their disagreements. After Steven and Ann married, when Molly decided to put all three in private school, Steven protested he couldn't afford to pay the tuition. "You have two incomes now and no other dependents, of course you can afford it. Anyway, it's a much better school. Evan especially needs to be in a more supportive environment, a place where he can get the help he needs for his dyslexia."

Molly trained her bitterness on Ann, too. which made it very difficult for them to develop their own independent emotional ballast. If anything, Ann thought, one more reason the sale of the house would be salutary

It is now so dark in the house that Ann must find her way to the pantry, to the overhead light there, to look at her watch. Six o'clock. She had told them she'd meet them at the restaurant at six. Faintly illuminated now by the pantry light, the keeping room's corners hold deep pockets of darkness. The fireplace, cavernous, is vaguely threatening.

In the front hall, casting a last look around the room before turning out the light, Ann catches sight of something, a faint gleam, in the corner nearest the kitchen. Paper towel? A corner of the damp mop? She crouches down for a closer look, realizing as she does so that her own shadow is blocking the light from the front hall. She pats the floor and the corner, seeking the object with her fingers. It feels like paper, wedged into the corner between the floor and the wall. Pulling on it gently, Ann finally wrests from its place, a piece of paper, folded in a triangle.

To examine it, Ann takes it into the pantry, where she discovers that the triangle opens up to reveal a four-inch square, formed of pockets that themselves open up to reveal crudely printed words. Ann smiles. She recognizes this, having made many of them as a child. The object is what she and her friends called a "cootie-catcher," with each panel of the folded square numbered from one to four so that the fortune seeker could pick a number and learn her or his fortune. Ann remembers that these included "fortunes" such as "You'll marry a millionaire and become a world-traveler," "The next time Bobby Chandler chases you at recess, he'll trip and break his neck." Such as they were, the fortunes Ann and her friends devised for each other were firmly grounded in the practical. After all, if one married a millionaire, one *could* become a world-traveler, couldn't one?

When Ann tries to open one of this cootie-catcher's compartments to read the message it contains, it begins to tear along the folds. She is able to see it better now by the pantry light, and observes that the penciled message is very faint, and the paper yellowed and very brittle to her touch. Clearly this is a relic of the past. But, she wonders, of her family's past or that of the previous owners?

She manages finally to open the pocket numbered "1" and reads: "You'll skip the fourth grade and Mr. Hancock will be your fifth grade teacher." Ah, the beloved Mr. Hancock! The teacher who designated Friday "pizza day." Everyone who finished her or his week's homework could partake. Those who didn't, couldn't. It worked like a charm. Most Fridays, during the regular lunch period, everyone sat down to enjoy the pizzas served in Mr. Hancock's classroom. So, Ann realized, this must be Zoe's cootie-catcher, since by the time Evan and Lauren reached fifth grade, Mr. Hancock was the school's principal. Friday was still pizza day, and the homework rule remained unchanged. However, now everyone in the school participated in the deal.

When Ann opens the pocket numbered "2," she reads: "Your allowance will be increased to $2.00." Two dollars! A fortune then to

Zoe, a child who saved every penny, earned or found. The message in pocket number "3" reads: "You will begin riding lessons in the Fall and your grandmother will give you a horse for Christmas." Ann remembers how desperately Zoe wanted—and bargained hard for—riding lessons. Like most horse-crazy 10-year-olds, she had longed to ride every day, through meadows and fields like those described in the horse stories she loved. Molly had made light of her passion, telling her that "horseback riders" didn't get into Radcliffe, her alma mater, and designated even then to become Zoe's as well. Zoe had to content herself with occasional visits to two elderly thoroughbreds, living out their last years in a paddock next to a friend's home in Bonny Doon.

When she opened pocket "4," the last one, Ann expected to find something to do with Zoe's 10-year-old interests, her passion for flea markets, maybe. With Ann, Zoe visited flea markets and antique shops every summer looking for porcelain boxes to add to her collection. Ann had given Zoe her first, a hinged box from Limoges, "certainly from the 18th century," according to the antique dealer who sold it to her. Whether it was or not made little difference to Zoe, who had fallen in love with its oval shape, and the pastel landscape painted on its cover. It just fit in the palm of her hand, and she carried it everywhere. She was eight.

"Your stepmom will die and your parents will get back together." Ann rereads the prediction. 1978. The summer Ann discovered the lump. Somehow, Zoe, ten at the time, had found out. Although she and Steven had agreed not to tell the children when they visited for the summer, Ann had wondered if Zoe, at least,

had overheard them discussing the biopsy, hoping for the best outcome, fearing the worst. At eight, Evan had no interest in figuring
out his parents and kept his distance from Ann. And Lauren, six,
was still very much the baby, clinging to her father, and periodically
lapsing into baby talk to express her need and dependence.

In the laundry room, folding sheets and towels, Ann listened to
Evan upstairs in Lauren's room.

"Make your bed! Pick up your room! Put the dish in the sink!"
He stamped the floor for emphasis. "She's not the boss. This is
Dad's house, too!" Beneath the scuffle of shoes and slamming
drawers, Lauren's response was inaudible.

Before the children's first summer in Newport, Ann and Steven
discussed and agreed on house rules. Steven, a high school teacher,
had signed up to teach summer school. Ellie, the eldest, had a
summer job bussing tables. So Evan and Lauren were with Ann
during the day. She didn't wonder—or even care, really—if they
would have been more cooperative—or less resentful—if she and
Steven had exchanged places. She knew he would be lenient with
them, because he was their father, because he knew they reported
back to Molly about what they saw and heard, and because he
abhorred nagging. They hoped they would outlast her, that their
mother, Molly, would return one day.

One time that summer, when she reminded Evan to take out the trash, he wheeled on her, screaming, "You can't tell me what to do. You're not my mother."

Steven told her often that rebellion and acting out were normal. "They're at that age where everything parents say or do is wrong, or meaningless, or stupid." He laughed. "They'll outgrow it, believe me."

"But I'm the wicked stepmother, remember?"

"Definitely not wicked, sweetheart." He hugged her. "Give them time," he told her. "They'll come around."

Ann had met Steven at a friend's party in Santa Cruz. At the time, she had been researching an article she was writing for "American Family" about single parents. Steven, who had recently divorced, showed her pictures or Zoe, Evan, and Lauren, describing how he had reorganized his life in order to spend time with them.

"I used to be able to be with them just by living in the same house. You know, I was present. I was there for them whenever they wanted me." He looked down at the floor, as if searching for something he had lost. "Now, I have to make a plan, pick them up, take them out, or at least, take them to my new place."

"Where are you living now?"

His lips thinned in a rueful smile. "I have a one-bedroom apartment. At Lakeside. When they come for overnights, they sleep on the floor in the living room in sleeping bags. Sometimes, when I get up at night and look in on them, they remind me of homeless people sleeping down by the river. They curl up like that, too."

He sipped his drink. "It must sound like I'm married to my children,"

"More like you miss them very much, that you're doing the best you can," Ann told him.

"I 'm afraid that's not good enough."

Later, remembering their conversation, Ann realized he hadn't mentioned Molly.

Several weeks later, after they'd had dinner together a couple of times, Steven organized a Saturday family outing to the aquarium in Monterey. In the back seat, Evan sat, playing with his Etch-A-Sketch. In the aquarium, he drifted from display to display, eyes cast down, ignoring even the jellyfish. Two years later, when Steven told them he and Ann were going to get married, Lauren and Zoe hugged her. Evan ran out of the room.

"He'll get used to it—to our being together, I mean," Steven assured her. "He'll come around."

Molly had custody of the children. When Steven and Ann moved to Newport, they stayedwith her in the 40s bungalow Steven had bought when he and Molly had first moved to California. Molly, an OR nurse, worked fulltime now that the children were all in school. Zoe, twelve, made sure Evan and Lauren got ready for school on time, did the laundry, kept track of their schoolwork, and their afterschool activities. Molly picked up groceries on her way home from the hospital and prepared dinner. Housekeeping was a casual affair.

"Do you think Molly will remarry?" she had asked Steven at the end of their first year together.

He shook his head. "It wasn't just that she didn't like being married to me. She didn't like being married. Period. One of her colleagues, another OR nurse, once told me that the best OR nurses are wedded to the job. They are single-minded, devoted, and not very good at sharing. They are addicted to responsibility."

"Just like surgeons?"

"I guess. Molly doesn't need a co-parent."

"No need for one, right? As long as she has Zoe."

Steven shook his head. "I'm not comfortable about that, but what can I do? I tried talking to Molly about hiring a housekeeper, you know, someone to come in three days a week, just to maintain the place." He shook his head and shrugged. "Anyway, Zoe seems all right with the arrangement. She's doing well at school. And Lauren and Evan do what she tells them to do."

"Up to a point," Ann said, not meeting his eyes.

"Even if I thought Molly would hear me out, I can't see any way to change things now."

Soon after this conversation, Steven applied for the position of vice principal at St. Steven's School in Middletown, Rhode Island, a job that included teaching AP history. Within six months, the school offered him the job and he and Ann visited together to look for a house.

Ann and Steven had lived in Newport since they married. This was the children's fourth summer with them, a summer, as usual, of confrontation and sulks. In three weeks, they would return to Santa Cruz, and Ann and Steven's life would revert to normal. She hoped the memories of this summer, like a bad dream, would soon fade.

Upstairs, Evan's rant continued. "He should make the rules, shouldn't he? He's our dad, isn't he? She's not our mom! She's a WITCH-bitch!!" A crash, breaking glass.

Evan and Lauren took the stairs two at a time, through the dining room to the kitchen and out the back door.

From the living room window, which looks out over the lawn and garden and the path to the street, Ann watched Evan, 10, and Lauren, 12, jostle each other and their bikes through the gate to the street, free at last.

Upstairs, in Lauren's room, the brass table lamp lay on the floor, bulb smashed, lampshade askew, but otherwise intact. Ann placed it back on the dresser, swept up the broken bulb, then vacuumed.

Alone at last at her desk, she pulled out the article she was revising, sipped her coffee, now cold, and sighed. She got it. She understood the children's anger and resentment, understood she was the only safe target. The divorce was now five years old, just one year older than her marriage to their father. They were its victims. But so was she, Ann thought. She was also the victim of her own illusions. Which was why every summer, when they arrived for their annual visit, she hoped it would be different, that she and the children would finally find common ground. Weeks ahead of time, she planned things to do with them—berry picking, the summer fair, picnics at the beach. She rehearsed lightening up, cutting them slack. If only it were that easy. No matter what she tried, Evan and Lauren found ways to redraw the battle lines, ambushing her determination.

With Zoe, now 14, it was different. From the beginning, Zoe seemed to understand Ann's tentativeness with all of them. As the eldest, she already had a habit of helping around the kitchen, encouraging Evan to "get a move on" when, distracted by a toy or a puzzle, he dithered.

The front door opened and closed.

"Hello? Steven?"

"It's me," Zoe calls. "Finished early today." That summer, Zoe was a part-time busser in a restaurant at the edge of the yacht harbor. She regaled Ann with stories about the other staff and the tourists. Yesterday she had told Ann about the couple whose baby had pitched handfuls of her food in all directions. Only her parents had ignored her. Zoe had offered them a table outside, which they cheerfully accepted.

A born peacemaker from the beginning, Zoe, then 8, had been willing to give Ann a chance.

Back in the kitchen, Ann poured another cup of coffee. Sitting at the kitchen table, the sun shining through the dogwood branches through the window behind her, Zoe was reading a letter. As soon as Ann sat across from her, she folded and pocketed the letter. "From Mom," she said.

"So, what's up?"

"The usual," Zoe answered. "She reminded me I should try to get a tetanus shot before I come back. And Ev and Lauren need to be sure to bring all their socks home this time." She laughed. Ann nodded. Molly had rules too.

"Ev and Lauren took off a while ago. To the park, I think." She decided not to tell Zoe about the broken lamp. What was the point? Zoe raised her eyebrows, as if she knew Ann was leaving something out. But Ann had made an effort from the start not to involve Zoe in her difficulties with Evan and Lauren, not to make her choose sides. So she wouldn't tell her about the lamp, or Evan's mockery.

"How was your morning? Any more food-slinging two-year-olds?"

Zoe laughed. "Nope. Today's prize goes to the guy who asked for eggs, sunny-side up, and sent them back when Josie, his waitress, brought them out."

"Why?"

"He said he'd asked for eggs over easy.'"

"What did Josie do?"

"She's so cool, Ann. She took his plate back, handed it to Dan at the grill, told him what she wanted, and he turned that order around in no time."

"Brilliant. That's a short-order cook for you."

"Was it true?"

"What?"

"That he'd ordered eggs over easy?"

"Nope. But Josie knows better than to argue. She needs the job."

The phone rang. Ann picked it up, smiling at Zoe, preparing to hand it over to her. Zoe's social life amazed her.

"Mrs. Davidson?"

"Yes?"

"This is Sergeant Drimmer at the police station. We have Evan here. Can you or your husband come down right away?"

"Of course, Sergeant." Zoe's face questioned the alarm she heard in Ann's voice. "Sergeant??" she mouthed.

"I'm on my way." Ann hung up, started to talk, but Zoe interrupted.

"What's going on?"

Ann pitched her voice as low as she could, to reassure her. "Don't know ... something. The cops have Evan." Zoe pushed back from the table, eyes wide, jaw tight.

"I'll come with you," Zoe said. Ann wanted to say no, but Zoe's expression cut her off.

"Let's call your dad, so he can meet us there, OK?"

Later, Steven would assure her that Evan's escapade—10 broken gaslights thanks to the boy's slingshot—is typical 12-year-old shenanigans, no big deal. Would she please just calm down? Fueled by wine and fatigue, Ann listened to herself, shrill and drunk, yelling, "No big deal? No big *deal*? For God's sake, Steven...!!"

Evan had been banished to his room; Lauren, watching TV, refused to talk about what happened (was she there or not?); Zoe is out with friends. Steven and Ann had paid a fine.

Because it wasn't the first time Evan had been in trouble, he had to do twenty hours of community service, too. As usual, Steven tried to talk things out; as usual, Evan stonewalled. For the next three weeks, counting down the days to their departure, Ann spoke only when spoken to, absorbed without comment Evan's and Lauren's provocations. She even withdrew from Zoe.

On the day they left for the airport with Steven, Zoe had hugged her; Lauren had brushed by her out the door. Evan had ignored her.

It didn't surprise Ann that the children might hope their parents would reconcile. Lauren and Evan had expressed this desire, either overtly, or by acting out. Evan, at age six, had challenged her: "Do you want to be my friend?" When she had quickly, enthusiastically answered him, "Well, sure!" he had replied, "Then don't marry my dad." For her part, Lauren, then three, would pitch hour-long screaming, kicking tantrums whenever she arrived for an overnight or a weekend with Ann and Steven.

What shocked Ann was that she had had no inkling at the time that Zoe, too, might hope that her parents would get back together, or that her hopes might be expressed in this way. She and Zoe had hit it off from the beginning, even before Ann and Steven had decided to marry. Zoe had imitated Ann's hairstyle, sat close to her when she read the children stories, so close that Ann had to wrap an arm around her in order to be able to hold the book open for all to see. She had also confided in Ann about tiffs with her best friend, sought comfort from Ann over real or perceived slights she experienced with other school friends. In fact, Zoe had accepted Ann in Steven's life and made room for her in her own. Had Zoe been acting a role, so anxious for her father's approval that she faked emotions she didn't feel? Was a 10-year-old capable of such duplicity?

Ann remembered that summer very clearly, because of her illness, especially because of her and Steven's fear of how the tumor she had discovered would affect their future. When they talked about it, it was as if they were discussing a problem child, one whose attitude and behavior was out of control, like the tumor itself, growing out of bounds within her breast. The only way Ann and Steven could discuss it and plan what to do about it, based upon the options presented to Ann by her doctors, was by objectifying it. However Ann, knowing all the while that she was talking about a part of herself, realized that she must accept the tumor in order to be cured.

In the shower, she avoided washing her right breast until the last minute, when she would lightly run her fingers over the breast, trying not to feel the lump as she did so. When she and Steven made love, she asked him not to touch her there, telling him this was practice for later if she had a mastectomy. "If they have to remove it, I don't want to feel its absence. Please, Steven, give me this." Although her request troubled him, she knew, Steven had complied.

Both of them had been stunned to learn that Ann would have to sign a release at the time of the surgery to remove the lump, so that if he found that the tumor was malignant, the surgeon could remove the breast immediately. Ann could not imagine now, let alone then, what it would have been like to emerge to consciousness following the procedure to learn that her right breast had been removed. Ann recalls that she and Steven didn't even consider opposing this procedure, or seeking a second opinion. At the time, it seemed their only recourse.

By the time the lump was removed, by the time it was discovered to be a benign fibroma, she had embraced the fact that it existed within her flesh, that it had been growing there, undetected, for some time, and that once it was removed, her most important job would be to heal herself, physically and emotionally. This knowledge was hard won. She and Steven had talked daily late into the night in the weeks before the surgery, working toward it together.

Ann had always been vain about her breasts. She had small, round, firm breasts that didn't call attention to themselves. They didn't bounce (feminist though she was, she always wore a bra) nor did she show them off in revealing clothing. To Ann, her breasts epitomized her physical self: compact, toned, fit. As she and Steven tried to accept the lump in order to deal positively with its treatment, Ann remembered talking about herself to Steven in ways she had never talked to anyone else.

"When I feel good, I feel intact. I feel that my skin fits me, and that I fit into the air around me. This lump makes me feel as though I've got a rough edge. To get back in tune, I've got to remove it, like a hangnail or something."

"Sort of like a splinter that you smooth out before you varnish a piece of wood?"

"Yes, like that."

"Well, does this make it easier to think about the surgery? Going through it? The surgery will remove the splinter?"

"Yes, but what if removing the splinter makes things worse, makes a hole that wasn't there to begin with, you know, I mean if they have to take the breast off. That means more roughness, more friction between my skin and the air around me. How will I deal with that?"

Steven was silent for a moment, then answered, "You're getting close to accepting the lump as a part of you. Can you take the next step, and accept the hole as a part of you too? Can you at least imagine accepting it, and bringing it into your sense of intactness? Besides, we don't know yet that they'll have to remove the breast. We don't know if it's cancer, Ann." Until now, Steven had been very careful not to say the word "cancer." Of the two of them, he was the optimist, always stressing the positive side of not knowing.

"I don't know how I'll deal with it if it is, Steven. I just don't know."

During the four weeks between her discovery of the lump and its removal, Ann felt detached from everything except the process of coming to terms with her illness. That the three children had had less than her full attention was undeniable. Was wishing for Ann's death Zoe's way of expressing her anger at what she perceived as Ann's neglect?

The summer visits were always stressful, especially at the beginning. As much as Ann, Steven, and the children themselves looked forward to being together every day for ten weeks, it usually took several weeks before they had established a daily routine that all could accept and live with. And every year they were challenged anew to figure out exactly what that routine was. In fact, life with the children changed year by year, as they themselves changed.

At that time, mealtimes were difficult for all of them—they rarely ate sit-down meals with their mother, and Steven had insisted that they eat dinner together, so that they could learn to talk to one another and to Ann and Steven. Somehow, this always turned into teasing one another to tears (usually Evan teased Lauren and Zoe teased Evan). Once the teasing began, Ann and Steven's efforts to have a conversation with any one of the three quickly changed to disciplining them all. During the weeks before her surgery, Ann dreaded these encounters to such an extent that she often begged off after preparing the meal. Thankful then that Steven understood, Ann now realized that her absence from dinner had sent the wrong signal: Look how easy it is to get rid of her! Just act up!

The day before her surgery, Ann told the children that she was going to the hospital for a checkup and would stay there overnight.

This was the best-case scenario: If the tumor turned out to be benign, Ann would be released from the hospital the day after her surgery. She announced her news just before they went to the beach so that it would be swallowed up in the anticipation of the day ahead. As Evan and Lauren ran out the door, Zoe, standing in the kitchen, looked at her. "What kind of checkup?" she asked.

"Oh, you know, I need to have some blood tests and a physical. Remember the physical you had before you went to camp last year? Like that."

"Yeah," Zoe responded, "but I didn't have to stay in the hospital."

"Well, I'm going to do that because this is the way it works for grownups. Anyway, you'll help Daddy make dinner, right? And you and Lauren can make chocolate chip cookies for dessert, OK?" Zoe nodded without looking at Ann and went to find her bathing suit. Lauren and Evan were already in the car, clamoring to go. Later, Steven reassured Ann that Zoe was fine, and that her reaction was the reaction of an intelligent, curious 10-year-old who was learning that adults don't always say what they mean.

At home after the operation, Ann recovered quickly. Like a sailboat running before the wind, she was buoyed by the euphoria that began the moment she had learned the tumor, a fibroma, was benign. Her surgeon and her doctor assured her that there would likely be no recurrence and that, in any event, this type of growth was not a harbinger of cancer. Once the bandage and sutures had been removed, she marveled that the incision was barely three-quarters of an inch long, skillfully incised around the breast's areola.

For the remaining six weeks of that summer, Steven spent as much time as possible with the children, shouldering Ann's responsibilities in addition to his own. Although even Evan rebelled at last against the steady diet of toasted-cheese-sandwich-and-soup lunches and McDonald's dinners, the children appeared not to mind that Ann infrequently joined them for their afternoons at the beach or for dinner.

Ann wonders now what she had missed. Not only in Zoe's behavior, but in Evan's or Lauren's. Were there signs that they knew how afraid she and Steven had been? Could they, like dogs and horses, have sensed this fear, even though Steven and Ann had put their best face on it?

Had Zoe, in fact, overheard their late-evening conversations? This would explain why she, at least, wanted to know more about Ann's hospital stay. It would also explain why she might have assumed that Ann had a life-threatening illness. Now, Ann would like to know. Whether Zoe would remember, whether she would answer Ann's questions about what she remembered, were issues Ann could not resolve without talking to her.

Ann's cell phone rang. Startled, she fumbled to find it in her bag, turning the bag and its contents upside down on the floor.

"It's me."

"Oh, Zoe, I'm so sorry. I've been here in the piano room since you left, just day- dreaming. I had no idea it had gotten so late..."

"It's OK, Ann. I'm just calling to find out what's happening, and also to let you know that Jake is going to be late." Ann understood that Zoe had suppressed "too." A stickler for punctuality herself, she was now the only family member who cared about being on time, a trait she and Steven had shared, making them the butt of numerous lame jokes.

"I'll have to thank him for getting me off the hook! But, Zoe, don't worry, I'm wrapping things up. I'll be there directly."

"OK. Jake should be here by then, too. I'm fine. I don't mind waiting. It's been a good break after all the moving commotion."

"I'll be there pronto, I promise."

"OK, Ann. Bye."

The question was, should Ann give Zoe the cootie-catcher? Doing so would lead to a conversation about it and, of course, about the message in pocket number "4." Would Zoe, now 32, remember how this message came to be written? Indeed, did she write it, or did one of her friends? Usually, Ann remembered, the fortune teller's predictions resulted from a giggled collaboration between the person for whom they were intended and the person who eventually manipulated the cootie-catcher and read the predictions aloud. What would be gained by sharing this find with Zoe? What did Ann really want to know? What would it mean to her to find out now that Zoe had wished for her to die, or at the very least, to leave Steven, so that her parents might have the opportunity to get back together again?

Of course, Ann realizes that her need to know what was behind the prediction has to do with what she called "step-parent limbo."

After more than twenty-two years as their step-parent, she is never really certain where she stands with Zoe, Evan, and Lauren. She knows even now that they do not accept her in the automatic way that children accept—and discount—their natural parents.

However, the most difficult times she had faced with them had come during their adolescence and early twenties, a time when even natural parents wonder who these strangers, their own children, are. During those years, they had accused their father of always "giving in" to Ann, of being "led by the nose." At one point, Evan, in a fury, had shouted at Steven, "Why don't you stick up for us? Why don't you do what *you* want to do? Why do you always do what *she* says?"

Now, they are young adults, with full lives of their own. And, although Lauren and Evan remained emotionally dependent upon their father, most of the barriers they had once erected against Ann had fallen. Or so she thinks. But because they have never really talked about their relationship—a topic all three children abhor—Ann cannot be certain of this. Perhaps she has grown so accustomed to the very formalities of their interactions with her that she no longer feels the strain, or, rather, the strain has become normal.

Ann knows she must make up her mind about whether to give Zoe the cootie-catcher and deal with whatever may happen as a result, or throw it into one of the trash bins on the curb. What will she learn about herself, or even Zoe, if she gives it to her? If what Ann wants is to find out how Zoe really feels about her—now, not twenty-odd years ago—there are surely other ways to do this.

Besides, since Ann herself harbors mixed feelings even today about all three children, her desire to force Zoe to declare herself betrays a hostility toward Zoe that Ann simply does not feel. Once she puts Zoe on the spot, it is conceivable, likely even, that Zoe's explanation of her wish for Ann's death will not have anything to do with the truth, which is what Ann is seeking. Or is it?

Is it possible that by wanting to force the issue with Zoe, Ann is looking for something denied her as long as Steven lived? That what she really wants is to sever relations with Zoe and, probably, with Evan and Lauren? She is becoming aware, just now, that that is the logical outcome of giving Zoe the cootie-catcher. For, after all, by giving it to Zoe, Ann is in effect saying that Zoe's past feelings about Ann matter more to her than her present feelings. When Ann considers how much effort over time has gone into forming their relationship, she knows that she cannot do this.

Ann makes one last pass through the house to make certain all the windows are shut. The front hall light dimly and indirectly illuminates the living room and den. Now the house feels as empty of memories as it is of furniture, as though Ann's efforts to interpret and understand Zoe's toy had so focused her recollection of what took place here that all other memories have been driven out. Still, Ann thinks that the decision to throw the cootie-catcher away, and not to press Zoe on what it meant, is an extension of her promise to Steven not to sell the house right away. To confront Zoe now about how she felt about Ann more than twenty years ago might expose flaws in their present relationship, flaws that Ann would prefer not to know about. It is far too likely that, once laid open to the light of her scrutiny and analysis, these flaws would be difficult if not impossible to fix.

In the front hall, Ann glances up at the windows overhead. Ensconced at the center of the web it has spun there, a tiny spider rocks gently back and forth in the breeze from the open front door. Stepping out to the first step, Ann closes and locks it behind her.

Good Enough

In January, I launched my campaign. "It's like plowing marshmallows," I told Mom. I had to dismount and push my two-wheeler on its fat balloon tires uphill and watch as my friends passed by on their racing bikes. "Besides, I've outgrown it." If I didn't curl my toes, they scraped the ground on the down stroke.

My birthday was April 3. I had four months to convince my parents to give me the 10-speed Schwinn I'd seen at the bicycle shop. "It'll last the rest of my life," I reasoned, hoping this approach would convince my parents I was mature enough to be trusted with a racing bike.

Mom looked at Dad.

Dad, reading the paper, gave it a little shake. "We'll have to see, Dana."

Opening and closing cupboards; the smell of coffee, bacon, and pancakes; Alex and Nick were in the kitchen, laughing and teasing one another. The ordinary sounds and smells of an ordinary school day. Except this was no ordinary day. Today was my birthday.

Below my window, around the patio, blooming daffodils and tulips bobbed in the morning breeze under the dogwood. My gaze stopped at the gate: A blue panel truck was parked in the driveway at the foot of the front steps. Two men stood behind it, opening the doors.

"Hurry up, Dana," the boys yelled up the stairs.

They giggled when I came into the kitchen. "What?"

"Not 'sposed to say," Nick muttered.

"Not say what?"

"Shush, you two." Mom came out to the kitchen and closed the door to the front hall behind her. With a warning look at Alex and Nick, she served my pancakes and bacon. She smiled as she put my plate on the table. "Happy birthday, sweetheart." She kissed the top of my head.

Nick and Alex finished their pancakes. "Can we go now, Mom?" Alex asked.

"When Dana's done." Mom handed a puzzle to Alex and a coloring book to Nick. "Be patient, boys."

I heard men talking in the front hall and the sound of wheels rolling across the floor. It sounded more like a dolly than a bicycle. Maybe the bike came in a crate that they brought into the house to unpack? I caught Mom's eyes. She smiled at me and turned around to put the boys' dishes in the dishwasher. Nick looked up from his coloring book and reached across the table, making an airplane noise, pretending to dive at my plate.

"No way. My birthday, my breakfast."

"Hurry up, slowpoke," Nick piped up. "We want to see your special present."

So did I. I ate the last bite of pancake and bacon and swallowed the rest of my orange juice. When Mom finished clearing the table, she pulled a scarf from her apron pocket. "First, the blindfold."

"Blindfold?"

"Because this present was too big to wrap."

Mom led me into the living room and removed the blindfold. As soon as my eyes adjusted, I looked around. "What happened to the bike?"

"Bike? What bike?" The boys hooted and laughed.

Mom put her hand on my shoulder. "Take another look, Dana." Her voice quavered.

Instead of a British racing green 10-speed Schwinn parked on its kickstand in the living room, there was a grand piano. Like an enormous gold and brown butterfly gleaming in the spring sunlight spilling into the room, the piano stood in the alcove, its strings and pale blond sound board reflected in its open lid.

Alex and Nick crawled under it, laughing. "Can we make a fort?"

"This was Mama's piano, Dana," my mother said. "Grandpa wanted you to have a real piano, so he sent it to New York City, to the Steinway company, to have it rebuilt for you."

I inherited my middle name from my grandmother, Elizabeth Hanaford, who had been a pianist. I had several boxes of her music, and a photograph of her playing this piano, which I kept on a shelf next to my upright piano in the den. I closed my eyes and imagined her, her hands on the keyboard, about to play. It was as if she were alive now in the room with us.

Mom cleared her throat and blew her nose. "Wouldn't you like to try it out?" I knew there was only one answer to this question. I sat on the leather-padded bench. Something in Mom's expression, both fearful and expectant, alerted me that more was required, but I didn't understand yet what that was.

I found Beethoven's "Für Elise" in one of my grandmother's boxes and learned it on my own to surprise my piano teacher, Mrs. Parker. After I played it for her the first time, she went over the score measure by measure, noting my grandmother's fingering and pedal marks, pointing out the diminuendos and crescendos and repeats. We both laughed at the exclamation points my grandmother had penciled in, reminders to pay attention. Thanks to Mrs. Parker, my grandmother, and Beethoven, I discovered that learning to play a piece of music involved more than getting the notes right. Much more.

Five years later, a month after my thirteenth birthday, Mrs. Parker moved to California with her daughter and her family. At our last lesson, she gave me a plastic bust of Beethoven. There was a small bookcase next to the piano in the alcove. I put Beethoven on the shelf next to the photograph of my grandmother. In it, dressed in a long-sleeved, floor-length gown—dark blue velvet, my mother told me—a white orchid pinned to the shoulder of her right sleeve, her hair in a braid coiled around her head, she sat at her Steinway, hands positioned on the keyboard. Eyes closed, head bowed, she was in a world of her own.

"Beethoven and your grandmother. From now on, you'll be playing for them both," Mrs. Parker told me.

After school, I sometimes placed Beethoven's bust and the photograph on the music stand next to my music. I'd play a scale, then stop and look at them. Speaking in a low, gruff rumble (in English, of course), Beethoven would urge me to slow down. My grandmother, her voice just like my mother's, would tell me it sounded "just wonderful." Then she'd suggest I play the scale again, three octaves this time, in triplets, starting pianissimo, building to fortissimo, then diminuendo back to pianissimo. Beethoven liked it that way too.

After Mrs. Parker left, my mother looked for another teacher. At the end of the summer, right before school started, she told me she had scheduled an audition for me with Mademoiselle Arnaut.

Born in Paris, Mademoiselle had studied with Debussy at the Paris Conservatory. She only accepted serious students—the ones with Juilliard or Curtis stamped on their foreheads. Even kids who didn't take piano lessons knew about her.

"She'll never take me. I'm not good enough."

Mom ignored me. "She has one opening. Your audition is next Monday."

Today was Wednesday. "I'm *really* not good enough, Mom."

"How do you know, Dana?"

"Because Jimmy's one of her students." Jimmy Bauer and I were the same age. He had played Chopin's étude in C minor, the "Revolutionary Étude," at last year's fall talent show. Kids had cheered. He'd begun lessons at three and practiced five hours a day. He was talented and conceited. And he'd had a crush on me since fourth grade. Besides, I knew something Mom didn't know. Although I liked playing the piano, I could take it or leave it. I wasn't a "serious student," like Jimmy. I knew my mother had her heart set on my continuing. She had made up her mind. I had never forgotten her reaction the day the piano arrived. She wanted me to become a "serious student," to follow in my grandmother's footsteps.

"I told her how long you'd studied, that you just turned thirteen. She seems to think you're advanced enough."

"What does she want me to play?"

Mom knew better. "Anything you want, is what she said."

After hearing a recording by Walter Gieseking on the radio, I'd learned to play Grieg's "The Butterfly." It had been my going-away gift to Mrs. Parker. I knew it by heart and enjoyed playing it. What did I have to lose, after all? Maybe the spirits of Grieg, my grandmother, and Mrs. Parker would carry me through. Anyway, it didn't matter—to me—if Mademoiselle Arnaut didn't accept me.

"I'll play the Grieg, then."

This was my first audition. The more I practiced during the weekend, the more my fingers skidded and slipped. Sections I'd played flawlessly just the week before fell apart. Muscle memory and music memory collapsed.

I barely slept Sunday night, playing the piece over and over in my head, battling my nerves (those butterflies swirled through me as if they had nothing better to do). Just before I got up, prepared to tell my mother I would rather die than play for Mademoiselle Arnaut, Jimmy Bauer's smiling face popped into view, provoking an adrenaline rush that overrode my panic attack: I would succeed with Mademoiselle, if only to prove to Jimmy that I could.

On Monday afternoon, on the way to Newport for my audition, Mom and I didn't speak. Glancing at me from time to time, she gripped the steering wheel with both hands. She was nervous, too. I made myself look out the window at the breakers pounding Easton's Beach, at the seagulls wheeling above the surf, at a boat—fishing boat or lobsterman—on the horizon. My butterflies began to settle.

"Even if Mademoiselle doesn't accept me, Jimmy will find out I auditioned," I told Mom.

"Let's get through the audition, shall we?"

"We, white man?" This was one of Nick's favorite lines. We laughed.

"If you study with Mademoiselle, you'll soon play as well as Jimmy, maybe even better." She patted my shoulder.

Mademoiselle had an apartment and her studio on the second floor of a three-story Victorian house near Newport harbor. Built by a local doctor in 1899, converted into apartments in the 1920s, the house towered over the two-story, eighteenth-century clapboard cottages that huddled around it.

Mom rang the bell. When a buzzer sounded, we opened the door into the entryway, which rose three stories above us. A trompe-l'oeil trumpet vine climbed its walls. Butterflies and hummingbirds flitted among the orange blooms or perched on buds all the way to the third floor. Mom raised her eyebrows at the butterflies and grinned at me.

Standing at the banister of the second-floor landing, Mademoiselle waved us up the stairs. Five feet tall, birdlike, her short, permed hair dyed reddish-brown, she wore a pale pink sweater, a calf-length tweed skirt, and a silk scarf loosely knotted around her neck and draped over her shoulders. Her eyebrows were plucked. She had penciled them in, and her eyes were heavily outlined in black. Mom explained later that this had been the French fashion when Mademoiselle was in her twenties.

On the landing, two small armchairs and a table with stacks of *Paris Match*, *l'Express*, and French *Vogue* sat to the left of the studio door, which was ajar. I could see the tail of Mademoiselle's piano, its back to the door, its lid open wide.

Mademoiselle shook my mother's hand, then gestured at the chairs and the magazines. "Please, Madame. You will wait for us here."

"First, listen. Then, talk," she said as she ushered me into the studio.

Mom smiled and blew me a kiss. I didn't give her a chance to hug me.

In the studio, shelves of books and music scores lined two of the walls. Framed botanical prints and paintings—Paris street scenes and a few landscapes—hung above the sofa against the wall to the left of the door. Across the room from the piano, a bay window with a window seat looked out through the branches of a large maple tree to Newport harbor, a block away.

Mademoiselle took my jacket and laid it on the sofa. She nodded at her piano, a medium grand. "My Steinway was built in 1936." She patted it and smiled. "One of the best."

I thought about my own Steinway (built in 1919, I wanted to tell her), and my grandmother, and Beethoven, waiting for me at home. The butterflies began to settle.

Mademoiselle pulled out a straight-backed chair and set it down to my left—close enough to watch my hands, far enough not to get in my way. "You may begin."

That she hadn't asked what I would play for her surprised me. My nerves shifted into high gear again—this time in anticipation of showing her how much I loved the piece. If I didn't play well enough to meet her standards, so be it.

She sat motionless, holding a small notebook and fountain pen, as I adjusted the height of the bench and ran my hands lightly over the keys, the ivory brighter—because newer?—than those on my piano. Without asking, without hesitating, I played a B-flat scale, a G-Major scale, then several arpeggios to warm up. The action felt stiff, the tone, even in the upper register, warm and mellow.

A bird called. Outside the window, a cardinal perched on a branch, head turned toward me. I began.

Mademoiselle shifted in her chair, leaning forward, listening.

I played the "The Butterfly" without a single fluff; its dreaminess and lightness seemed muffled, perhaps due to the carpet and drapes. When I finished, I waited as Mademoiselle wrote in her notebook. Except for an occasional passing car or the sound of her pen, the room was silent. How many others had sat like this, waiting for her to pass judgment?

When she looked up at me, there was something in her expression, something about her eyes, as though I had her full attention. "That's a lovely piece," she said. "I've played it often. Once for a recital when I was a student at the *Conservatoire*." She smiled, her eyes half-closed. "Many people assume these pieces—the ones in the collection, I mean—are *faciles,* that's to say 'easy' for beginners. But, you know, they are not at all 'easy' pieces." She shook her head.

Her mocking laugh passed judgment on the "many" who were, in her view, simply wrong.

"Who are your favorite composers?" she asked.

"Bach. Beethoven. And Schubert. And Chopin." My voice sounded older, confident and relaxed. "And Ravel."

She didn't ask what pieces I knew by heart, or which ones I had played and why I liked them. This wasn't a conversation. She was evaluating my attitude. Was I serious enough to merit her time and attention?

"Do you like to sight-read?" Under the penciled arches of her eyebrows, her brown eyes focused on mine, bright and birdlike.

"I don't know."

"You don't know how?"

"Is it something you have to learn?"

"Oh my, yes." She made another note. "Who is your favorite pianist?"

I listened to recordings on WGBH, the classical radio station in Boston, and my mother took me to concerts at Symphony Hall and recitals at New England Conservatory.

"Rudolf Serkin, Vladimir Ashkenazy, Horowitz. And Madame Darré." I knew she wouldn't ask, but I longed to tell her about Jeanne-Marie Darré's performance of Chopin's Ballade in g minor at Carnegie Hall, about the notes rising in clusters, like schools of brilliantly colored fish, up to where I sat in the balcony.

She closed her notebook and placed the cap on her pen. "*C'est bien, alors.*" She smoothed her skirt, gave her scarf a little tug, and gestured at the sofa. "Please." She crossed the room and opened the door. "Please, Madame. You may come in now."

Mom sat next to me on the sofa and patted my hand. In the armchair, Mademoiselle crossed her ankles and reached behind her to adjust the cushion. "She plays quite well, your daughter, considering her training," she told my mother, paging through her notebook. "And she is musical. If she works hard, she could be quite good."

Sometimes, alone at home, practicing, I fantasized about playing in Carnegie Hall, imagining the applause and the calls for an encore. I tried various versions of my bow and my stage smile in front of the full-length mirror in the upstairs hallway. But I knew it would take more than bows and smiles to be a concert artist. The nausea that overcame me at the very thought of performing in public anywhere, let alone Carnegie Hall, left my hands wet, clammy, and inert.

On the way home, I cried. "'Quite good'? It's like I said, Mom. I'm not good enough."

Mom fished out a tissue for me.

"Be patient, Dana. She'll send a letter, she said. Someone like Mademoiselle—"

"You mean, someone whose students all play like Jimmy?"

She pushed on. "To Mademoiselle, 'quite good' may be the next-to-last stop on the way to 'very good.' Look, Dana, if you were already 'very good,' you'd be enrolled in the NEC Preparatory Program, and we'd be living in Boston." Stopped at a red light, she looked at me.

"If she doesn't accept me, then what?"

"I'll keep looking."

Because Mom had her heart set on Mademoiselle Arnaut, I couldn't tell her that was fine with me.

The acceptance letter arrived the following week. I reread Mademoiselle's comments for the umpteenth time, trying to figure out why what she said didn't make me feel better about my playing. What was missing? I was "promising," "a hard worker," "musical," she wrote. She didn't say I was talented. Even I knew that talent was what set "serious" apart from "good enough."

"She could tell from the way you played that you practice, that you work hard," Mom said. "Give yourself a chance."

I didn't dare tell Mom what I knew. Or that I had hoped Mademoiselle wouldn't accept me. That afternoon, I sat at the piano, holding my grandmother's photograph, trying to imagine what she was thinking, trying to imagine what she would advise me to do. She had been a talented musician. That much I knew. But I also knew she had stopped playing the piano. I didn't know why. Did she, too, suffer from the fear of not being good enough? I remembered something Mrs. Parker had told me.

I'd been struggling with a piece, something by Bach. I kept making the same mistake. In frustration, I pounded the keyboard. Mrs. Parker took my hands in hers and held them while I cried.

When I calmed down, she talked to me about how much she had wanted to become a concert pianist, how, in the end, she realized she would never be good enough to be a star. "I didn't have the talent. And besides, I wanted other things in life, like marriage and children. As a concert artist I'd have spent most of my life travelling, concertizing." She smiled. "I knew if I did that, playing the piano, which I loved to do, would soon become drudgery. That was unacceptable. But I continued to study the piano and eventually became quite good at it. I enjoy playing. And I enjoy teaching. That's good enough for me."

I decided to go ahead with Mademoiselle. I knew I would become a better pianist. It didn't matter what I chose to do with it in the future. Not yet.

At first, my lessons with Mademoiselle felt like walking on thin ice. She never smiled, never encouraged me. Sometimes she would stop me as soon as I began and have me play the same phrase over and over throughout the hour. No matter how much I practiced, it seemed I couldn't satisfy her. But I didn't want to disappointment Mom, even though there were times I wished for a broken bone, or a fatal illness—anything to avoid my lesson.

One day, a rainy March afternoon, I arrived a few minutes late for my lesson, prepared to spend the hour reworking the same passage. I played the Schubert Impromptu I was working on for the annual recital. Halfway through, I realized Mademoiselle was listening, eyes closed, leaning back in her chair. Usually she sat up straight, scrutinizing me. I played the last chord. And waited.

"*C'est très bien*, Dana. Very good." Quickly she went over the score, pointing out places that still needed work. None of her comments got through to me. All I could hear was, "*C'est très bien*, Dana."

She was sixteen years old when she played Debussy's "Clair de lune" for Debussy himself at the Paris Conservatory, where she was a student. He told her he couldn't have played it better. "That was my proudest day," she said, looking down at her hands. She had been a rising star until a bicycle accident shattered her left wrist.

Mom hugged me when I told her. "That's what she saw when you auditioned. You can do this."

Mom was right about one thing, at least. For months, I'd been learning how to practice. And becoming good at doing what I was told. "You must pay attention all the time," Mademoiselle admonished me. "If you don't correct your mistakes right away, they will follow you wherever you go, whenever you play—for me, or anyone else. Slow practice, hands separate, first. Then slow practice, hands together. You're training your muscles, yes. You're also training your brain. If you do this right, they won't let you down." Her eyes narrowed. "You must listen to yourself, Dana. Mistakes only happen when you're inattentive." Did she realize she was rubbing her wrist, the wrist she had broken when she fell off her bicycle?

The system worked for me once I began to play more complex pieces. Analyzing and practicing phrases, linking them, helped me to develop my technique—and to memorize. With each new piece, I became more confident.

But the more confident I became, the less I enjoyed playing. I didn't begin to understand why until two years later, after the competition.

My sophomore year of high school, the piano competition application arrived in February. After work, before she made dinner, Mom came into the living room with a cup of tea. Distracted, I fumbled at the keyboard.

"How's it going today?"

I was working on Debussy's "Clair de lune." It terrified me. I couldn't stop thinking about Mademoiselle playing it for Debussy.

"Not so great. I screw up something different each time I play it through." It takes time to build muscle memory, time to know the structure of the piece so well, it's as if you had composed it yourself. So far, this ease had eluded me.

I ran my fingers over the keys, smooth, cool, and inert. Sometimes they felt smooth, and fluid, like flowing water. At others, they felt like ice floes separated by uneven gaps, crashing together as they raced down a turbulent river.

Mom cleared her throat. "Mademoiselle thinks it would be good for you to enter the competition this year," she said. "You'll start preparing now; then you'll have the summer." Her eyes brushed over me, checking my reaction. "You'll have time for your schoolwork, of course. But nothing extra."

The idea of playing for strangers was about as appealing to me as having my fingernails pulled out. When I played for myself, for Mom, or for Mademoiselle, my butterflies perched, quiescent in the shadows. So far, I hadn't been able to admit to my fear of playing in public—not to Mom, and certainly not to Mademoiselle.

"What about my job?" I enjoyed my part-time summer job at the library—two, sometimes three hours shelving books every weekday afternoon. It wasn't as boring as it sounds, because I got to check out new books and walk to and from the library, along the beach. Usually, I took my Walkman and listened to recordings of pieces I was working on. Mademoiselle wouldn't have approved. But she didn't know. What I knew is that it helped me hear the pieces without having to think about them. Someone else was in charge. I could relax and enjoy the music.

"We'll have to wait and see if you have time for that."

I decided not to push my luck. "Wait and see" might work this time.

"What about Jimmy?"

"What do you mean?"

"Will he be competing?"

"Of course."

After my first month of lessons with Mademoiselle, Jimmy had cornered me in the cafeteria. "How's it going, Dana?"

"Fine."

"With Mademoiselle, I mean."

"That's what I meant, too."

"She's pretty easy, at least at the beginning."

"Really?" Ignoring his smirk, I walked away.

Thanks to Mademoiselle, I learned to enjoy practicing. Everything that was new and out of control in the beginning eventually settled into a state of comfort and familiarity once I'd mastered her method. The steps to connecting the notes on the page to my fingers on the keys resembled dissection. Having dissected a frog, I knew about muscles, tendons, and joints, how they worked. So, the mechanics weren't a mystery. But there was more to playing a piece of music than mastering the hands-together issues and memorizing the music.

The summer before the competition, I practiced for two hours every morning, working my way through each of the three selections, checking fingering, dynamics, and tempo. This was a mostly mechanical exercise.

Then I met Jean.

On my way home from the library every afternoon, I passed Joe's Café. Weathered siding, wraparound deck, and college-age wait staff—it was one among several bars and restaurants opposite the beach on East Main Road. It was the only place that featured live music daily from midafternoon until midnight. Joe, a retired jazz bassist, had connections. And an interest in promoting young musicians.

One afternoon a tune I didn't recognize played by a virtuoso accordionist—a fast two-step—spilled out Joe's open door. I went up the steps to the deck and peered in. The singer's voice dived and swooped over his accordion. He was accompanied by a fiddle, a guitar, a bass drum, and what appeared to be a washboard. The guy playing it ran a spoon up, down, and around it, producing a rhythmic, raucous clatter. It was a "frottoir," I learned later, an instrument traditional to zydeco and invented in the United States.

Dressed in a muscle shirt and jeans, the singer, dark-skinned and built like a dancer, hopped and stamped around the stage, shoulder-length dreads bobbing, arms pumping the accordion, fingers racing up and down its keyboard. His glossy baritone blended with the fiddle tune, weaving around and through the accordion's accompaniment.

By the time the band took a break, a small crowd had joined me on the deck, clapping and dancing. Wiping his face with a towel, the singer's eyes met mine. He put the accordion down on a stand and said something over his shoulder to the band.

On the steps as the crowd broke up, he introduced himself. "Name's spelled like Jean, but it's pronounced Jon," he said, pronouncing the "J" with a "za" sound. "Buy you a drink?"

"Iced tea?" I smiled so hard my face hurt.

"I can handle that." He had a hint of a French accent. Unlike Mademoiselle's, his was warm and soft, a drawl; hers was prickly, like the wind in your face.

He went back inside. The phrase *da capo al fine,* "take it from the top," was tattooed across his shoulders. In classical music, this phrase cues the musician to repeat a section from the beginning (*capo*) to the end (*fine*). So this guy, Jean, an ace accordionist, was also a classical musician?

He handed me my iced tea and sat down on the steps with a cup of coffee. "You from around here?" His tone of voice, his half-smile, told me he knew the answer.

"What about you?"

"Martinique, Baton Rouge. And Boston. I'm a junior—NEC, the conservatory."

I nodded. I was right about the classical music part. "So this is just a summer job?"

"The drummer knows Joe. He's in one of my classes. He got the gig. The accordion player he signed up had to go home. So, here I am. At your service, mamzelle." He pretended to doff a hat and grinned.

I wondered how Mademoiselle would react if I called her "mamzelle."

"You like zydeco?" He asked as if he knew the answer but wanted to hear it anyway.

"Zydeco?" My tongue prickled, as though I'd eaten something peppery.

"What we've been playing." He sipped and savored his coffee for a moment before swallowing. "It's Louisiana Creole music."

I shook my head.

"It's kind of French. My family's kind. Zydeco? Long story; a lot of history." He gave his dreads a shake and smiled. "I'll tell you about it sometime." I smiled at his certainty there would be another time.

He stood and tossed his empty cup into the trashcan.

I looked around. A few people, summer people, sat on the hoods and bumpers of cars, waiting for the break to end.

"I've got half an hour," he said. "Can I give you a lift?"

"Okay." My head spun as if there'd been something stronger than lemon juice in my iced tea.

Jean waved at his motorcycle, a blue Suzuki parked under a tree. "Your ride, mamzelle." He removed two helmets from the seat. "Room enough for two."

I put on the helmet and got behind him. Everything slowed down. Zydeco. Louisiana Creole. Jean and his motorcycle. Up close, his skin gleamed; the tattoo rippled when he moved his arms. I would have asked him to take the long way home, but there wasn't one.

"S'okay to put your arms around me," Jean said. "Or you can hang on to my belt." He laughed, gunned the motor, and headed out of the parking lot, away from town and Joe's. The drummer tipped his hat as we rode by.

The fragrance of wild roses and the brackish scent of the marsh followed us along the beach, past sunbathers and volleyball players.

Too soon, Jean downshifted and turned up our driveway. Mom, at the kitchen sink, looked out, then disappeared.

She met us outside the gate. Jean parked the bike, removed his helmet, and shook out his dreads. Mom didn't move. Or smile.

"This is Jean, Mom."

Jean smiled at her and held out his hand. "Jean Lemaitre."

As she shook his hand, Mom looked him up and down, as if making mental check marks: skin color, muscle shirt, dreads, and the Suzuki. *Wait 'til she sees the tattoo.*

"Hello." My mother stared past him across the road.

"Very pleased to meet you," Jean said.

"Would you like to come in, Jean?" I started toward the house.

Mom stepped toward me, between us. "I left some green beans in the colander, Dana. Would you wash them? And set the table? I'm going to pick up your father."

Jean put on his helmet. His back to my mom, he winked and smiled. "Au revoir for now, Dana." He let the bike coast down the driveway, turning the engine over when he reached the road.

"A tattoo? Really, Dana?"

There was no point trying to explain then what I knew about Jean, what the tattoo meant about him. I'd have my chance later, when my father came home.

A half-hour later, my parents came into the kitchen. Mom dropped her keys on the counter and crossed her arms. "A stranger on a motorcycle?"

"He's a musician, Mom. He's got a summer job at Joe's."

She glanced at Dad, lips faintly pursed.

"He brought me home, didn't he? I even wore a helmet."

Dad poured a drink. Mom shook her head. "He's at least twenty-three. And he's not from around here."

Jean would have to be at least nineteen to play at Joe's Café. Maybe he was twenty, since he was a junior at NEC. But he wasn't twenty-three. Still, I knew better than to argue the point.

Dad loosened his tie and sipped his drink. Mom didn't bring up the dreads. Or that Jean was black. I could tell she already had.

"Dana." Dad's voice came out low and tight. "You signed the contract, honey. No dates in cars until you're seventeen." Dad, a lawyer, thought contracts were the solution to every problem. You read the terms; you agreed to the terms; you signed on the bottom line, accepting the penalty for non-compliance.

"A ride home isn't a date."

Mom's look said, "I told you so."

"Really," she said. "For the rest of the month, I'll pick you up from the library." She tapped the counter for emphasis. Dad drained his glass.

Mom often bragged that she never had to worry about me—unlike Alex, who never met a rule he didn't challenge. Two years older, I learned early that doing as I was told made my mother happy. I'd never crossed the line before.

Later, lying in bed, I thought about *da capo al fine* and about going back to the beginning, starting over, with changes along the way—changes I would choose for myself. I couldn't relive the last sixteen years. But I could start paying attention to what was going on behind the scenes, who I was becoming, and learn how to make changes that mattered to me, first.

In the morning, I found a note from Mom on the kitchen table. "I'll pick you up at 4:30. Wait for me." I crumpled it up, tossed it in the trash, and spent the morning practicing. At noon, I walked into town, to the library, wondering if I'd see Jean again. He must have picked up clues from Mom's behavior toward him. I cringed, remembering her look, a look he couldn't have missed.

Jean and the band weren't at Joe's yet, so I didn't stop.

Two blocks from the library, I heard the motorcycle behind me.

Jean stopped and got off. "Was it bad?"

I nodded. I couldn't look him in the eye.

He smiled. "First time?"

I nodded.

"The bike?"

"Yeah. Plus, they think you're too old for me." I didn't think my parents were prejudiced. Probably it was the combination of all Jean's differences that earned their disapproval. Probably, if I hadn't accepted the ride, if I had brought him home and introduced him like any other boy they hadn't met, they'd have been more accepting.

"How old are you?"

"Sixteen."

He let out a long, low whistle and smiled. "S'okay. We'll deal." Pushing the bike along, he walked me to the corner, just out of sight of the library's front door.

"No use advertising it, right?" He nodded toward the library, touched his finger to his lips, and ran it along my cheek. "Later." Halfway up the block, he turned and called back to me, "Nineteen!"

At dinner, Dad did his best to distract us. "Remember Mrs. De-Witt?"

Mom puffed out her cheeks in a little sigh.

"Her neighbor is trying to sue her. Again." Loud laugh. Too loud. "Same reason, of course. She leaves her dog tied up outside all day and it barks nonstop." Big sigh. Shrug. "So, here's what the judge did. He told Mrs. DeWitt he'd have her dog repossessed if she didn't keep it indoors."

Mom sipped her wine, patted her lips with her napkin. I kept my head down.

"Don't you get it?" He glanced at Mom, then at me, as if we didn't already know how hard he was trying. "You can't have a dog repossessed. It's not like a car. But the threat did the trick. He's something else, that judge." He chuckled and got up.

Mom pushed her chair back.

I cleared the table and loaded the dishwasher.

After I'd gone to bed, they sat on the patio talking about Shelly, my mother's sister, who had run away with Marco—on a motorcycle—when she was seventeen. Marco had been twenty-three. Even the FBI got involved in the search.

"I had to go home for a week the month before I graduated from college to help find her. Never again, Daniel."

"Dana's not Shelly, Anne." Dad's tone, soothing, placating, drifted up to me.

The patio's screen door slammed. My cheek still tingled where Jean had touched it. In the moonlit sky above the trees outside my bedroom window, he floated, whispering, "S'okay. We'll deal."

Beyond the French doors open to the patio, the garden shimmered after a night of fog. Even the piano keys were damp. I dried them one by one and let the piano case air dry. Mom and Dad had left early to spend the day in Boston with friends.

The surf pulsed faintly under the call of the mockingbird that nested in the magnolia tree in our garden. Alone in the quiet house, I warmed up with scales and arpeggios, then began to play the Debussy waltz "La plus que lente," one of the three competition pieces. For the competition, I would play only one of the three. I wouldn't know which one until I walked out onto the stage, where a judge would announce it.

With Mademoiselle, before I began to learn a piece, I studied the score, which she had marked up: fingering (in pencil), the dynamics (red for *forte*, blue for *piano*), learning where phrases began and ended, identifying fingering challenges and tempo changes, listening to it in my head. Some pianists listen to recordings of different interpretations as they begin to work on a piece. Mademoiselle frowned on this. The interpretation she knew, the one she passed on to me in her markings on the score, was always her own. Except for "La plus que lente." She assured me her interpretation was Debussy's.

"You must hear the music in your own head, Dana," she told me. She pronounced my name "DahNah." "If you listen to recordings, you'll just imitate what you hear. And if you have a memory lapse? What happens then? If you haven't been listening to yourself all along from the very first time you played the piece, you'll be lost."

I understood what she meant. But to make it work was a challenge. Too often, what came out of the piano wasn't at all what I heard in my head. Today was one of those times. So I stopped. I couldn't fix what was wrong by repeating the same passage over and over.

I had just closed the score when Jean cleared his throat. He stood on the patio, helmet in hand.

I waved him in.

He put his shoes next to his helmet on the mat by the door and came over to the piano. "May I?" He leaned over the soundboard, as if listening to its secrets. Of course, I told him about my grandmother and showed him the photograph. "Before he died, my grandfather had the piano restored for me. For my eighth birthday."

He let out a low whistle, "That's some birthday present."

Only the soundboard and ivories hadn't required work. While I was telling Jean the story, he wandered around the room, pausing at the shelves of trophies on the near side of the fireplace.

"Your brother's?"

"Alex's yes. He's the older one."

"And the younger one?"

"Nick is an artist." I had never said this before. None of us had. For the first time, I realized it was true. This was Nick's truth. "He did those pen-and-ink drawings."

The drawings represented different flowering plants—an epimedium, a sunflower, a Japanese iris. The detail of every leaf, stem, and petal gave each plant such depth and texture, each one appeared three-dimensional. Mom had once called Nick's drawings plant portraits. Seeing them now through Jean's eyes, I understood what she meant.

Jean took a closer look. "You can feel the leaves, smell the fragrance almost, can't you?" He turned and gestured at the piano. "I've got an idea about that passage you're working on. May I?"

It was as if he'd read my mind. I hadn't had a lesson since Mademoiselle had left for France. She'd prepared a detailed practice plan for me, but it didn't answer my questions. Especially, I needed the reassurance I heard in Jean's voice—reassurance that I didn't have to do this on my own.

"Please."

He sat to my left on the bench, close but not touching.

"Hold my arm, right there." He positioned my left hand just under his right elbow and began to play the passage I had been working on without looking at the score. The weight of his wrist and forearm lay loose and free in my hand as he played the first phrase.

"See? When you settle into the keyboard, you get this open, full sound." He turned, straddling the bench, motioning to me to do the same. Holding my right wrist in his left hand to steady my arm, he positioned his right hand on my forearm, lifting and dropping each finger, one at a time, his wrist relaxed. My skin tingled.

"Your turn." He swiveled back around and inched over to his left to give me more room.

I started to play, linking the weight of my arm through my wrist and hands to the keyboard. I could feel the difference; hear it, too. The tension in my neck released. Now the waltz melody seemed to swing over the accompaniment. And my touch was secure in the keys from the moment I began. I took my time going into the downbeats—even my breathing slowed—as I finished the phrase.

"You're pretty good at this, you know?"

Mademoiselle's comment that I played "quite well" still resonated, a reminder that being "musical" wasn't enough. If I was "pretty good" in Jean's eyes, though, that was good enough for me.

"What do you see when you're playing this piece?" he asked.

"I don't understand."

"Let me play it for you. Close your eyes. Let your mind drift. Remember that Debussy called this a slow waltz—actually, a slower than slow waltz. He wanted you to understand that we're not in Vienna, that this isn't a Strauss waltz. It's more of an impression of a waltz. Like a dream or a memory. It's up to you, the pianist, to recreate that impression, so that the listener can see and feel it."

I sat on the sofa, eyes closed, listening to Jean, imagining dancers moving across a stage or a dance floor, the men in waistcoats, the women in ball gowns, swaying as they circled the floor, their shadows floating like petals on the surface of a pond, brushed gently by the breeze. I began and played it through to the end, feeling the water, the breeze, the languid pulse of the dancers circling the floor.

"That's what I mean," Jean said.

"That was lovely," I responded.

"Duets?" He pointed at the cabinet where I kept my music.

"Take your pick."

We played Schubert, Mozart, and Brahms. By now, I knew how to sight-read well enough to enjoy the challenge. Jean hummed along or whispered encouragement. Every time my forearm brushed his or our feet happened to collide over the pedal, we adjusted. "It's like dancing, trying to remember—to feel—who's leading," I said.

Jean laughed. "That's one of the reasons I want to conduct."

"So you can lead all the time?"

He grinned.

Our music teacher at school conducted the school orchestra. We needed him to keep time, but there wasn't much else he did for us. Of course, what Jean was talking about was different.

At 1 o'clock, he stood and stretched. "Gotta go," he said. "You too, right?"

He had left the Suzuki parked at the foot of the driveway, leaning against the fence. He grabbed the handlebars and began to roll it down the driveway to the road.

On the way to town on the main road he told me about his classes—at Berklee and at NEC—and the gig at Joe's. He'd taken it for the summer to pay for Berklee, so his parents wouldn't know he'd enrolled in jazz classes there. "My father. He tried that life. Then, he met my mom. For her, it was a package deal. If he wanted to marry her, he had to find real work. Now he's an accountant. But he still plays, a little. Classical, now, that's a whole other story. That's what they want for me."

"So, conduct Beethoven, play zydeco on the side?"

He grinned. "That would work."

We stopped at the intersection near Joe's. Steam from the pavement swirled around us. As the fog lifted, the sound of the surf grew louder.

"Come to Joe's tonight?"

"My parents. Well, you know ..." I looked at him.

He smiled and brushed a strand of hair off my forehead. "I'll pick you up at your place and we can walk down together. It's only a couple miles. You'll be home before midnight. They'll never know."

When Dad called at six, I told him I'd practiced and gone to work, as usual, a half-truth that made my heart pound.

"We'll be home after midnight," he said.

I could tell he wanted to talk more, maybe ask what I had planned for the evening, but I didn't want to answer a direct question with a lie. "I'll be in bed by then." If all went as Jean and I had planned, this part, anyway, wouldn't be a lie.

Out of breath, as if I'd been running, I drank a glass of water and splashed some on my face, gasping as it spilled down the front of my T-shirt.

The piano lid was still open, as we'd left it that morning. I sat down and played Chopin's "Revolutionary" étude, its runs and arpeggios rising and falling like rollers cresting and then breaking on the beach. When I finished, I laughed. Some revolution.

Jean knocked on the back door at nine. Thanks to the fog, the porch light glowed in a misty halo. We felt our way down the driveway and along the dirt shoulder. Occasionally, he reached out and touched my arm, his fingers warm and dry. When we came to the first streetlight at Beach Road, he took my hand.

Joe's was packed. Mostly tourists, as far as I could tell. Except the group in the corner, sitting at a table behind the bar—Jean's band and their girlfriends, their eyes on us, as we crossed the floor. Like the other girls, I wore jeans and a sleeveless tank top. Unlike them, I was underage. They pulled over a chair for me.

As the band warmed up for their first set, I went to the far corner of the dance floor. I wanted to listen and dance, not talk. They started with the same two-step they'd been playing when I'd first heard them. The next number, a slow waltz, was a zydeco version of *"La plus que lente."* Jean's eyes searched me out. I waved and clapped when the fiddle eased into a bluesy rendition of the melody. As played by Jean on the accordion, the chords in the bass breathed into the downbeats. More than a variation, the band's version was an original, the way jazz renditions of familiar tunes always are. I would never again hear—or play—the piece without thinking of this one, this night.

Listening to this rendition of "La plus que lente," I thought about Jean's tattoo, *da capo al fine*, which I now saw in a new light. Every performance of a piece you know well, whether you play it or someone else does, differs from the previous ones. Exciting—and terrifying, when you're the performer. Anything can happen. I could learn the notes and develop my technique. But how could

I prepare for the unexpected? How could I make *da capo al fine* work for me?

During the first break, Jean found me and we went out to the parking lot. When he pulled me to him, his arms went around me just so, like when he played the first phrase of the waltz on my arm. What started out as a hug turned into a kiss that lasted until I broke away to take a breath.

Jean slid his fingers up the back of my neck into my hair, giving me a little shake. "Again?"

This time, I breathed with him.

At eleven thirty, the beginning of the next break, Jean waved me over to the back door. Arm around my shoulders, he guided me along the road toward home. We could hear the surf, the waves crashing, invisible in the fog. Thicker now, it transformed the streetlights, the neon signs, and the traffic lights into glowing smudges of gold, green, and red. Once again, we stayed on the dirt shoulder. In my sandals, it was like being barefoot.

"What do you want to do with the piano?" he asked.

"Just get through the competition, for now."

"Hard work." The smile in his voice carried through the fog.

"Bach, the Schubert Impromptu, Debussy, from breakfast to noon. And sometimes after work."

"Which Schubert?"

"Opus 142, no. 3."

He let out a long, low whistle. "One of my favorites."

I nodded. "Mine too, now. But I don't get it."

"What's not to get?"

"The whole program. I'm learning the notes. But am I learning the music?" Each piece held its own perils. "It seems like no matter how much I practice, every time I play a piece, it's the first time all over again." I had to ask. "Is that how it is for you?"

"Sometimes. What about your teacher? What does she think?"

"She's away for the summer."

We had reached the foot of the driveway, drenched and shivering. "I'll wait here 'til you're in the house." He kissed me on the cheek and patted my shoulder. "You start practicing at nine?"

"My parents leave at eight thirty."

"'Til tomorrow, then. Nine-thirty sharp."

At the front door, I turned to look for him. He had disappeared. A car came down the hill, fog swirling around its high beams as it slowed and headed up the driveway.

I kicked off my sandals and ran to the back door. Behind me, the car doors slammed. My parents laughed as they came up the front walk. I took the stairs two at a time in the dark, tiptoed down the hallway to my room, and huddled under the covers, out of breath, heart pounding. "You're pretty good at this, you know," I whispered. And giggled.

Thorough as it was, Mademoiselle's practice plan lacked one essential ingredient: there was no one who could listen to me and give me pointers while she was away. Sure, I played for my parents, but to them almost anything sounded "just fine, dear." So, when Jean offered to coach me, I didn't hesitate.

By unspoken agreement, we didn't discuss what (or if) I would tell my parents about our arrangement. If we timed Jean's arrivals and departures right, they'd never know. Most mornings, he arrived at nine-thirty, settled on the sofa with a cup of coffee, and spread the scores open on the coffee table. By then I'd had enough time to warm up and review what we'd worked on the day before. Every day, I varied the order, starting with the last piece I'd played the previous day and working backwards through the program. This had been Jean's idea: "You won't be in the habit of starting the same way. When you get to the competition, you'll be comfortable starting with the one they ask you to play."

Jean's suggestions for changes in tempo and phrasing helped bring each piece into focus. Mademoiselle had framed everything in terms of precision and clarity—crescendo to here, release pedal there. As if standing on a mountaintop, surveying the bands of color traversing the fields below, Jean saw how each phrase connected to the next, how the voicing could be adjusted in the repeats to bring out new features. This is how I learned the value of *da capo al fine* as a concept, and how I began to tame my fear of the unexpected.

"What isn't written down—ever—is that you're supposed to repeat the passage but not play it the same way. Sounds self-evident, right? We're not machines. The music lives and breathes through us. But it's deeper than that. You're supposed to make small changes in dynamics and emphasis. So the 'da capo' gives you a fresh start. Think of it like this," he said. "You're creating a soundscape, painting a picture in sound. Close your eyes for a minute. Listen." He played the Bach prelude through. "What do you see?"

I took my time. "There's water—a pond or a lake?"

"Clear sky? Clouds?"

"Slow-moving clouds reflected in the water." I opened my eyes. Jean smiled. "Play it."

When I finished, he clapped softly. "Slow-moving clouds, still water. All there, Dana. Just right."

The pond I imagined wasn't a pond I'd plucked from the gallery of ponds I knew. That wasn't the point. The effect of cloud reflections in the water's calm surface was. These were in the music. Now they were in me.

"What about the Schubert?" Jean flipped through the score and smoothed it open.

"Sometimes I feel like I'm in a maze. I get lost in the repeats."

"I hear that when you play it."

"What do you mean?"

"You're tentative, holding back, as if you're feeling your way. But, you know, you need to trust yourself more. You said it yourself: You know the notes. Now tell the story."

"I don't understand."

Jean motioned me over to the couch, spread the score across his lap and leaned back, his legs stretched out under the coffee table. "Schubert marks the score in all the usual ways—tempo, dynamics, phrasing. That's the easy part. The hard part? This is a theme and five variations. It's like having five different perspectives on a beautiful landscape. Pretend you're a movie director. This is the opening shot of your film. You move from a birds-eye view to a close-up in the sunlight, to a middle-distance view as the clouds pass, and so forth."

"I'll try that. Maybe that will help me with some of the problems."

"Technical?"

"Sometimes, I feel like I'm losing control."

"Which part do you like best?"

"The fifth variation."

Jean nodded. "Why?"

"It's fun." I laughed. "And it's the last one."

"Before you begin, remember that. It's a kind of homecoming." He placed his hand palm down on the score, his eyes holding mine, as if that way he could transfer to me the feelings he described so that I would feel them and convey them in my own playing. "One more thing. Every time you perform, you're meeting the audience for the first time. This Impromptu is a gift, a wonderful surprise. It's your job to unwrap it and dazzle them with what's inside."

The difference between his method and Mademoiselle's couldn't have been clearer. Mademoiselle emphasized mastery and control. Jean showed me how to make the music mine.

"You have it all, Dana"—he took and held my right hand, palm up, gently stroking it with his index finger—"here." He kissed my forehead. "And here."

One morning in early August, Jean sat next to me, working with me on a new fingering for a passage in the Schubert. I tried it out. It was like untying a tricky knot. Jean touched my arm. Mom had come in. She was standing behind the sofa, her shoulders rigid, mouth set.

Jean started to get up. I shook my head. He sat down.

"Come with me, Dana." Mom said.

I checked the clock on the bookcase. "We're almost done here, Mom."

"Now, Dana."

I didn't move. She left the room.

I played the passage again, up to speed with the new fingering, flawlessly. Twenty minutes later, Jean left.

Mom sat at the kitchen table, staring into space, holding a cup of coffee. "How long has this been going on?"

"All summer."

"Every day?"

"Almost."

"Why haven't you told us?"

"Because I knew you'd say no."

She went to the sink, turned the faucet on. And off. She leaned against the counter, facing me, hands in her pockets. "You're here alone. We don't know him or anything about him."

"I told you everything you need to know the first time you met him. He studies piano and conducting at NEC. Maybe you don't remember because you were paying more attention to the color of his skin and his tattoo."

"So he's a musician."

"A pianist, Mom."

"A pianist, then. How is he helping you?"

"If you promise to listen, I'll explain."

"I'm listening."

"Today, for instance, he showed me fingering that works much better for me in the Schubert."

She raised her eyebrows. Mademoiselle taught me the fingering she had learned, fingering passed down generation to generation. To change it was like denying God.

"And how to prevent wrist cramp," I continued. Mademoiselle's remedy? More slow practice. Which didn't help. "He showed me how to shift the weight of my arm off my wrist. Problem solved."

Mom nodded. Even she understood this. Then, "What will you tell Mademoiselle?"

"I hope she hears the improvement."

The sound of the surf, the birds in the garden, all the usual early afternoon sounds pooled around us.

"So that's it?"

"That's it?"

"Between you and your friend?"

"Jean, you mean?"

She pursed her lips. "Jean, yes."

I'd won the battle. I tried to see myself as she saw me: growing up, making my own decisions. I hoped she realized she could let me go, that I wasn't Shelly. I wasn't rebelling; I was trying to do my best. With Jean's help, I thought I might have a chance.

Once I had the pieces in my fingers, under control, the glitches smoothed out, Jean and I worked on my memory. During the last two weeks of August, he tested me, stopping me in mid-phrase, talking to me to distract me, then having me pick up where I left off. At first, I stumbled around, got lost, backtracked to find my place. Eventually, no matter where he stopped me, or how he distracted me, I could start over where I had left off, at will.

I no longer feared the competition. And I didn't care if Jimmy Bauer won. I just wanted to play as well as I knew I could.

I met Jean at Joe's on Friday of Labor Day weekend, my last day at the library, a couple of hours before his last gig. We sat on the bench across the street, watching a few windsurfers making the most of the light breeze.

He handed me a small, flat package wrapped in crinkly silver paper, tied with a blue ribbon. "You can open it now, if you want."

It was a CD in a blank jewel case.

"The guys and I made it for you. Our favorite tunes—zydeco, that is—whenever you need some sunshine." He touched my cheek. "Call me sometime."

We didn't make any promises. Or say goodbye.

"How many of you?" he asked.

"Eight. Four in the morning, four after lunch."

"When's your turn?"

"Right after lunch—which I'm not planning to eat, by the way."

"What will you do this morning?"

"Read the scores over, then warm up."

"And the butterflies?"

"Swarming."

He chuckled. "Remember what I said."

"Everything?"

"Remember to breathe, wise guy."

"That's my favorite part."

"What do you mean?"

"It's the only part that always works."

"Knock 'em out, Dana." His low, quiet tone held out to me all the energy and focus we'd built together over the summer.

"Talk to you later."

Whatever was unfinished between us would remain unfinished. I didn't know if I'd see him again. He'd said he might come back to Joe's next summer, but that would depend on his course work. There were summer school courses he could take, especially if he found a gig in Boston. He wanted to graduate early, because there was a conducting competition to prepare for. It was as if, like a piece of music transposed to a different key, we had transposed our relationship during our summer of working together. He might have been my boyfriend; instead, he became my coach. That was just the way it was.

Inhale as the adrenaline surges; exhale to let it go. Every day I had practiced this technique with Jean in the series of "startle" tests he dreamed up to condition me to handle my fight-or-flight reaction. These worked nearly every time. With practice, my hands and legs didn't tremble, my heart didn't pound, my throat didn't close.

I took a deep breath and checked the time. Three hours to go.

At the piano, I bowed to the four judges seated in the second row. The audience sat in the darkened auditorium behind them, invisible from the stage.

One of the judges, a woman, stood. "Good afternoon, Dana. We are looking forward to hearing you play Schubert's Impromptu, opus 142, no. 2. Please take as long as you need before you begin."

Wait 'til I tell Jean.

I adjusted the bench. Until I dried them with my handkerchief, my hands were so damp and cold, I couldn't grip the knobs. My pounding heart drowned out all other sound, except Jean's voice in my ear: "S'okay, Dana. Inhale. Exhale." I closed my eyes, heard the Impromptu's opening passage in my head, and began to play, listening to every note, shaping every phrase.

My problems with the Schubert began and ended with the repeats within each of the variations. The notes were the same, but the idea was to play them differently, different versions of the same material. Changes in emphasis helped, as if you were saying to the listener, "Here it is again, only this time, please notice the lovely bass line. See? It's the mirror image of the treble."

Near the end of the fifth variation—six measures, eight measures? —as if I'd missed a step on my way down an unfamiliar stairway, my mind went blank. My hands, inert on the keyboard in front of me, lay there, detached and unresponsive. *Do something. Play something. Play anything.* Hadn't Mademoiselle warned me? *If you stop listening to yourself, you'll be lost.* So I played a chord, something that sounded more like Bartok than Schubert. I had come to the end of the Impromptu and lost my way. I needed then to get off the stage, to escape from the dark, from my failure, from the audience, which only then began to stir. Scattered applause followed me off the stage.

It was over.

Mom and Dad waited for me in the corridor backstage. Dad took my hand. "It's okay, Dana. Whatever happens, whatever the results, you did fine."

I'd had my chance. There would be no *da capo al fine*.

We went out to the lobby, where Mademoiselle joined us. "Next time, it will be different. You'll see." She patted my shoulder, looking past me at my parents.

Jimmy, the last to perform, came out, triumphant, grinning. Juilliard had accepted him, early decision. If he won the competition, it would be a mere afterthought.

Half an hour later, we gathered in the auditorium—competitors, family members, teachers, and supporters. The judge gave a short speech about what an honor it was to serve on the panel, how impressed the judges were with our commitment and talent. "And now, it gives me great pleasure to announce our four winners. In fourth place, Ella Jenkins. In third place, Ross Michaels. In second place, Alice Anderson. And in first place, Jimmy Bauer."

I closed my eyes, imagining how I'd feel had I been awarded a ribbon, or even an honorable mention. Dad hugged me. "You'll have another chance, sweetheart."

Dad, Mom, and I went out to dinner, to the Crow's Nest, and sat on the deck overlooking the harbor. Everything, even the flourless chocolate cake, my favorite, tasted like sawdust. When the bottle of Veuve Clicquot arrived, Dad asked the waiter to pour three glasses and lifted his in a toast. He set it down, folded his hands in front of him on the table. "So, honey, what do you think happened?"

I shook my head. "My brain hung up on me, like when the phone goes dead." When I closed my eyes, I could still see my hands, the hands of a stranger, lying on the keyboard, white, helpless, still.

Mom and Dad exchanged a look. "We'll talk more later, Dana," Mom said.

"Dana?"

I held my breath in the dark. My door was closed. Maybe she'd go away. I didn't want to talk. I needed time, settling time, to get used to "after." "Before" was over.

She opened the door. "Dana? Sweetie?"

"What, Mom?" I sat up and switched on the lamp.

She sat in the armchair across from my bed, sniffling. "A story about your grandmother I want to tell you." She held one of my dad's handkerchiefs in her right hand, bunched against her chest. In her left, she held the photograph of my grandmother.

"Why are you crying?"

"You know that Mama stopped playing when Shelly was born." She blew her nose. "There's more to the story."

She took a deep breath and cleared her throat. "Before she got pregnant with Shelly, Mama had begun to work on a recital, her first public solo performance. It was hard for her after she got pregnant, but she didn't let up until she had to." Mom laughed softly. "Her belly got in the way." Mom smoothed and folded the handkerchief in her lap. "Then Shelly came. She was a breech baby."

"A breech baby?"

She took a deep breath and cleared her throat. "Born bottom first. They had to do a caesarean.

Shelly, my footloose, fancy-free aunt, nearly hadn't made it. On the dresser, I had a photo of Shelly and me at the beach. In a wide-brimmed sun hat, her blond hair blowing around her bare shoulders, Shelly laughs into the camera. She glows. her energy flows into the room.

"Papa talked her into postponing the recital for three months. The night of her performance, I wore a white organdy dress with a green sash. I can still remember the sound and feel of it, how it swished against my legs." She smiled. "It tickled something awful when I walked."

Mom held out to me the photograph of my grandmother.

"Mama bowed, went to the bench, and sat for a moment. I could hear Papa breathing, almost panting, next to me. She placed her hands on the keyboard and bowed her head."

I waited, imagining the scene, the rustle of the audience, settling, my grandmother in her velvet gown. Mom was crying again.

"Papa's eyes were fixed on her. As the silence grew, it seemed like hours passed. Then Mama got up and stepped away from the piano. She opened her mouth and made a sound, something like, 'oh,' or 'no,' and collapsed."

I held my breath.

"She was afraid she wasn't good enough." Mom took a deep breath, as if she were climbing a steep hill, preparing herself for the last push. "She had a breakdown. Eventually she was hospitalized. Chronic depression. She never played again, Dana."

Several weeks later, Mademoiselle reassured me that every soloist suffers memory lapses. It was just nerves, she told me. With more experience, I would learn how to improvise my way through, if it ever happened again.

I didn't tell her then that there wouldn't be a next time, that I had decided I would play the piano only when I wanted to, on my own terms. I wouldn't apply to the conservatory or compete, ever again.

At the end of my senior year, I told Mademoiselle and my parents that I'd decided to focus on writing and the sciences in college. Having made that decision, I returned to playing the piano as if visiting a place I'd loved long ago, a place I believed I had lost. It wasn't lost; it had been waiting for me all along.

All in Good Time

When the phone rang at 6:30 on Wednesday morning, Laura checked caller ID and braced herself. Ellen only called this early when she was in trouble.

"El?"

"I want a divorce."

Not "Jean-Claude and I are separating..." Not "Jean-Claude and I aren't getting along. Again."

"I want a divorce." Bridge crossed.

"You've been here before, El, remember the last time?"

"Of course." Ellen blew her nose.

That time, Jean-Claude had come home and announced he had had it with the "American system." He was ready to go back to France.

Laura sat on the stool by the phone. "I'm listening."

Ellen sniffled. "You really have no idea how bad it is. He's always on his best behavior with you and Mark."

"I have time now. Why don't you get a glass of water? I'll wait."

Laura heard the refrigerator door open and close, the sound of water pouring into a glass, Ellen blowing her nose. "I'm back." She cleared her throat.

"What's going on?"

"It's that instructor, the one who supervises his course. She's on his case all the time, according to him."

At the university, all foreign language instructors taught introductory courses. Responsible for guiding them, an associate professor was assigned to observe and evaluate them and report their performance to the department head. These reports could make or break a promotion.

Ellen sighed. "She is such a pain, Laura. For one thing, she interrupts him all the time. She even corrects his pronunciation."

"She's French, right?"

"Born and raised in Paris." Ellen made a sound between a laugh and a groan. "And that's a major part of the problem. Jean-Claude's accent, the Lyonnais accent, Is different. The course monitor corrects Jean-Claude's pronunciation in class. No wonder he's insulted and embarrassed."

"The students aren't aware of this are they?"

"Probably not. But Jean-Claude thinks she's putting him down. Apparently, she smirks when she corrects him."

"Has he talked to the department head?"

"Not yet."

"Why not?"

"In the French system, the system he's used to, you don't complain to the department head. It just isn't done. He hopes he'll have a chance to prove himself when she visits his class at the end of term.

"How could that help?"

"First of all, she's American and she'll focus on how attentive he is to the students—and how well he presents the lesson. Still, he worries that the course monitor's report might have a negative effect...that the chairman will be expecting him to blow it."

"Isn't there anything he can do in the meantime?"

"He's in such a bad mood all the time, we can't discuss it." Ellen sighed. "Anyway, that's not all."

"What do you mean?"

"The pregnancy business." Ellen's voice dropped. "We keep trying."

"What did your doctor tell you?'

"All the test results are positive. Everything's fine, according to her. We should try to relax." She sighed. "As if. With everything that's going on for Jean-Claude in his course, neither of us is relaxed about anything."

They had met during Ellen's junior year at the university, Jean-Claude's first year as an exchange student. To earn extra spending money, Ellen had tutored French students in English. Jean-Claude had been one of her students. "Not exactly a 'meet cute,'" she had told Laura, "But close enough." Two years later, they married, and Jean-Claude settled in the US.

Now, at the end of his third year in graduate school, Jean-Claude was working on his PhD in French literature. Ellen taught English at a private school.

Laura checked the calendar hanging beside the refrigerator. "We don't have anything going on this weekend. Why don't you come down here? Mark and Jean-Claude could hike up to the water tower. You know how much they enjoy that. Maybe it would help Jean-Claude to talk to Mark."

"I hate to put this on you and Mark," Ellen fretted.

"At least ask Jean-Claude. And put away the 'd' word, for a few days?"

"I guess I've seen this coming," Laura told Mark Thursday evening, after Ellen called to confirm that she and Jean-Claude would drive down to Newport on Saturday morning. "You know how prickly Ellen can be. Obviously, Jean-Claude's behavior doesn't make it easier. And these blow-ups keep happening."

"Maybe they should see a therapist?" Mark suggested.

Laura smiled. "I have another idea."

Mark raised his eyebrows. "You want me to talk to Jean-Claude?"

"Just sound him out. You two could go for a walk while Ellen and I make dinner."

"Lasagna?" Mark smiled.

For as long as Laura could remember, lasagna—her Italian grandmother's recipe—had been the family's comfort food in troubled times.

Saturday morning, as Laura mixed the sauce ingredients, she remembered helping her mother prepare Thanksgiving dinner the weekend Ellen had brought Jean-Claude home for the first time. Ellen had told Laura she wasn't in love with Jean-Claude (she had made air quotes for emphasis). She enjoyed his company, because they could talk about anything. "And I love his accent, of course. He sounds like he's purring."

Six months later, Ellen announced she and Jean-Claude had decided to marry at the end of their senior year. "We don't want a big wedding. We'll invite family and our best friends. It will be informal—no gown, no tux, a picnic lunch down by the lake after the ceremony." She smiled at Laura. "We'll have cupcakes and champagne."

"There will be vows and rings, at least?" their father interjected.

"Of course, Daddy," Ellen laughed. Jean-Claude's uncle, a goldsmith, had designed and made their rings.

Ellen and Jean-Claude arrived after lunch on Saturday afternoon. Standing at the kitchen sink, Laura watched them unload the car. Mark came into the kitchen and looked out the window. "Looks like they stopped at Whole Foods on the way."

"I asked them to pick up a few things," Laura told him.

Ellen entered the kitchen and set her shopping bag on the table. "Camembert and gruyere, two kinds of lettuce, and two baguettes. Ta-da!"

Jean-Claude followed, two bottles of wine in a string bag looped over his right shoulder, a pastry carton in his left hand. "Strawberry tart," he announced. The fragrances of cheese and strawberries wafted through the kitchen, blending with the tangy smell of the tomato sauce simmering on the stove.

Ellen leaned over the pot of sauce and inhaled, noisily. "Couldn't we eat now?"

Mark laughed. "Hike first."

Jean-Claude set the wine and the pastry carton on the kitchen table and sat on the bench beside the kitchen door, while he put on his hiking boots.

"Two hours up and back." Mark checked the clock over the sink. He looked at Laura. "Should be back by 4:30."

Laura smiled. "No rush." The sauce, simmering, would require occasional stirring until 5. She would cook and drain the pasta at 4:30, so it would be ready to layer with the sauce. There would be time to make a salad while the lasagna baked, and everything would be ready at 6:15.

As soon as Mark and Jean-Claude left, Laura brought out a plate of brownies and turned on the espresso pot. Ellen put the pastry and cheese on the counter and sat at the table. Outside the kitchen, a pair of blue jays squabbled. Filtered through the maple tree near the house, sunlight dappled the garden and lawn below.

"Have you and Jean-Claude talked any more about what to do?"

"Several times I've suggested he try to find a job in publishing." Ellen looked up at Laura. "There are three companies in Boston that publish foreign language textbooks. I think he'd be good at that, and that he'd enjoy it." She shook her head and sighed. "So far, he's determined to stay at the university, to finish his degree, come what may."

"Does he have any idea if he'll be promoted?"

"That's the problem, really. Although he's well-liked in the department, the woman who oversees the French course he teaches is very tough." Laura shrugged. "Maybe Mark can persuade him to try something else once he's finished his degree."

After parking the car, Jean-Claude and Mark walked down into the ravine at the far end of the parking lot, crossed the brook to the trail on the other side, and began their walk single-file uphill through the red oak forest.

"Any new information about what happened to the natives here?" Jean-Claude asked.

"They died out. That's all the latest research confirmed. Disease or something else?" Mark shrugged.

"Maybe conflict with another tribe? Or starvation?" Jean-Claude wondered.

"They've studied this site over the years," Mark said. "Aside from a few arrowheads, and bones—animal and human—nothing much has turned up."

"No significant clues, in other words?"

"Right," Mark nodded. "I guess they're trying now to link the settlement here with another one on the other side of the valley." He shrugged. "Who knows?" He smiled and added, "I come here for the walk."

Nearing the top of the trail, they climbed over a downed tree. Just over the rise, they reached the clearing and the fire tower. At the southeastern edge of the forest, it stood in the middle of only site with 360-degree views of the surrounding valley.

Gathered around the tower, excavated then left behind after the construction, a half-dozen rough-hewn granite boulders huddled, like ancient worshippers. Mark brushed one off and sat on it. Jean-Claude cleared a spot on the next one over. For awhile, they sat, silent, listening to the wind in the trees, the faint sound of traffic rising from the valley and the occasional clang of the cable around the rim of the tower's tank.

"Must be lunch time," Mark said, pointing to a single hawk soaring above the tree line, its hunting cry fading as it headed up the valley to the west. "I just read that adult hawks eat at least five to eight times a day." He looked at Jean-Claude. "They spend a lot of time hunting. It's a full-time job, really, a necessary one, too, when they have young to feed."

Jean-Claude nodded. "Not that different from us, I guess."

Mark sat back, looking up at the tower. "Another fifteen, twenty years, I bet the tower will be gone. Only people who still live around here then will remember it," he said.

Jean-Claude laughed.

"What's so funny?" Mark asked.

"You just put your finger on the problem."

"Animal or vegetable?"

"Existential," Jean-Claude replied.

"You mean, like the Indians, our time--our existence--is defined by who remembers what?"

Jean-Claude nodded. "Something like that. After all, nothing we do—and certainly nothing we say—lasts forever. I suppose, as teachers, we can hope that our teaching endures, at least if our students remember something of what they learn."

"When did you decide to go into teaching?" Mark asked.

"When I was sixteen, I did some tutoring." Jean-Claude looked down at the ground, at a twig lying beside his right foot. He leaned over to pick it up. "The boy next door was struggling to learn

English. I was advanced enough in my own English studies to enjoy the challenge of figuring out what he didn't understand and making up games to help him learn and remember."

"Seems to me there's a big difference between teaching English—for you, a foreign language—and teaching French—your native language." Mark paused.

Jean-Claude shook his head. "Not really. The rules may be different, but communication is communication, you know? What I enjoy is the interaction. Especially when the student develops confidence to take what he—or she—has learned and communicates a thought, or a request, or even 'Wha-wha-where's the washroom'?" He shook his head, looked away.

"What is it?" Mark asked. "What just happened?"

Jean-Claude looked down. While he'd been talking, he had peeled the bark from the twig. "Stutter," he said. "I've stuttered since I was a kid." Jean-Claude looked away. "Ellen knows."

"What about your colleagues? And your supervisor?" Mark asked.

"Not them. Never them, if I can help it." Jean-Claude tossed the twig across the clearing. "Lately I've hit a couple of bumps. Times when I slip, when the stutter comes back. It happens especially in class when the supervisor interrupts me."

"How do you handle that?"

"I cough, or I repeat myself, something I learned to do when I was younger. It sometimes helps to slow down. The problem is, when the prof corrects my pronunciation, she expects me to repeat right away. I've learned to cough, then repeat. Most of the time that works OK." Jean Claude smiled. "I'm getting better at it. Although my Lyonnais accent is still with me—no matter how hard I try."

"Why is that such a big deal?"

Jean-Claude shook his head. "Because we're snobs."

"'We'?

"We French, I mean," he laughed. "Any French accent other than the one you hear in Paris is considered déclassé."

"So, what can you do?" Mark shook his head.

"That's the problem. I've worked hard to soften my Lyonnais accent. But it's with me still, especially when I get excited or enthusiastic about something." He shrugged. "I'm making progress—I practice with tapes, and I record myself, you know, to learn which words give me the most trouble. I've improved a lot." He laughed. "But when the supervisor is in the classroom, my nerves trip me up." He shook his head, frowning. "I'm not the easiest person to live with when I've had a bad day at work."

"Can you speak to your department head about this?"

"Not yet. I don't want to seem like a whiner. So, I plan to talk to her at the end of the term. I'm going to suggest that she ask the prof who supervises the course not to interrupt classes with her suggestions."

"Do the students notice?" Mark asked.

Jean-Claude shrugged. "I'm not sure. But they have a hard enough time mastering the basics. Her comments on my presentation and her corrections disturb and distract me."

"Do you like teaching?"

Jean-Claude looked away, across the valley, as if summoning his thoughts, calling them back. His smile faded. "Not at the moment."

"Why is that?"

"For one thing, I want to teach literature, which is where I'm headed. For another, the prof's interruptions make it clear I'm not in charge. For example, I'll start explaining something to the students...," he shook his head. "I was about to add, '...and they just don't get it.'" He laughed. "Of course they don't get it. They're still learning." He leaned over and picked up another twig, "That's not the real problem."

"The prof, again?" Marks asked.

Jean-Claude nodded "She jumps in, interrupts me when I'm in the middle of an explanation."

Mark nodded. "That throws you off?"

"*Exactement.* Sometimes, she corrects my word choice. Sometimes she corrects my pronunciation. The students' attention shifts from me to her. They lose track of where they are and stop following me."

"Is she French?"

Jean-Claude sighed. "She's from Paris. I'm from Lyon. My accent is different from hers. You know, a bit like the difference between a New Yorker's accent and a Vermonter's accent."

"So she wants you to adopt a Parisian accent?"

"Exactly. I've tried. Most of the time, I'm okay. Unfortunately, when I'm speaking normally, explaining something, I revert to my native Lyonnais ways. She objects and corrects me, as if I were one of the students."

"Uh-oh."

"Exactly. It's demoralizing. And it confuses the students. At one of our weekly meetings, I asked her to write down her corrections and discuss them with me after class."

Mark nodded. "Seems like a good idea. What did she say?"

"She refused. She told me that on-the-spot corrections stick. After-the-fact corrections do not."

Mark nodded. "What are you going to do?"

"If I were single, I'd quit now and go back to France." Jean-Claude shrugged. "But that isn't an option. Or a solution. I'll stick with it until the end of the year, try to 'go with the flow.' I plan to go to the national languages conference in the spring, look for another position. Maybe something will turn up."

"What about trying to find a position in a private school?"

Jean-Claude nodded. "Ellen has suggested that, too. Or I might leave teaching altogether, find a position in a company that does business in France." He sighed. "I must keep this job for now, probably for at least another year. Ellen and I need our two jobs to survive."

"What does Ellen think about your situation?"

Jean-Claude shook his head. "I haven't told her everything. I want to have a plan, a solution to discuss with her. I can tell she's worried." He twisted the twig he'd been holding until it snapped. "I've been a bit of a boor, lately."

"A boor?"

"I've been in a bad mood, for weeks." He looked at Mark. "I really don't know what to tell Ellen. I was hoping I could sort things out myself, but that seems less and less likely."

"I'm certain she wants to help you," Mark said.

"Of course. The problem is, I need to help myself. That's who I am." He shook his head. "Besides everything else, my stutter seems to be getting worse." He stopped and looked at Mark.

"Is there someone you can work with on this?" Mark asked.

Jean-Claude nodded. "I have an appointment next week with a speech therapist. But that isn't the main thing."

His voice neutral, Mark asked, "What else is going on?"

"Ellen and I have been trying to get pregnant. So far..." Jean-Claude shrugged and hung his head. After a few minutes, he dropped the twig, brushed off his hands and rubbed them against his thighs. "We have an appointment in six weeks with a doctor who specializes in infertility. Ellen found her. It's too early to know if she can help us."

Mark drew a breath and leaned back, bracing himself against the warm stone.

"It must be hard to concentrate on preparing and teaching your classes," Mark said. "And grading," he added.

Jean-Claude nodded. "I'll have my review next month. That's when the department head visits the class."

"Will you have a chance to talk about your concerns?"

Jean-Claude shrugged. "I plan to write up some questions, just in case."

Both heard the hawk's cry and looked up, searching for it. "There it is," Mark said, pointing above the tower, beyond the tree line. The bird soared in a widening circle above them, chased by a half-dozen smaller birds.

"Crows," Mark said. "The hawk must have found their nesting place."

The crows darted around the hawk, as it shifted direction. Then, as if alerted by a common signal, they turned away, heading back the way they had come.

The hawk called once, then swooped across the valley out of sight.

"Years ago, when I was just starting out I took the first job offered me at Jones & Buckley, the publisher in Boston." Mark laughed. "They hired me as a proofreader, because I'd worked for my college newspaper and because I scored 100 percent on their test." He glanced at Jean-Claude. "After six months, they enrolled me in a copy-editing course." Jean-Claude looked puzzled. "The point is this: I didn't know anything about editing. But I was a fast learner. I focused on my assigned tasks and paid attention to the editor I worked for. You can't beat on the job training."

Jean-Claude smiled. "Sounds like you think I should stay the course."

Mark nodded. "At least until you've finished your dissertation. Besides, who knows who'll direct your teaching next year? Also, you'll be spending a lot of time in the library, researching your dissertation."

Jean-Claude brushed pieces of shredded bark off his lap. "That's the plan, at least."

"Will you continue teaching?"

"Of course."

"The same section?"

"Probably not. But I won't know until the fall."

"Can you speak to the chairman about what you'd like to do?"

"Sure. But he bases his decision on his needs. Until all the enrollment forms have been submitted, he can't finalize his plans."

"Best case scenario?" Mark asked.

"It will be my fourth year. I hope they'll assign me a section of the introduction to literature course." He shook his head.

"What is it?"

"If they consider my past record, my experience teaching in France, I mean, think I might have a chance at that one." He sighed. "But I don't know. The prof who teaches the course is working with several PhD candidates. He may pick one of them."

"Maybe you should talk to your department head next month, to see what your chances are?"

"You mean 'put my foot in the door'? Jean-Claude smiled.

"Make that 'get' your foot in the door," Mark answered. Both laughed.

"Since you're headed for your doctorate, and you'll be working on your dissertation next year, don't give up hope. Keep your eye on your goal."

A loud cry startled them. The hawk had returned. Above them, it wheeled sharply, following the crows down the mountain.